DANGEROUS HAREM

DANGEROUS HAREM

JOHN B. THOMPSON

CUTTING EDGE

This book substantially revised and re-released in 1961 as *Texas Tramp*.

ISBN-13: 978-1-957868-50-9

Published by
Cutting Edge Books
PO Box 8212
Calabasas, CA 91372
www.cuttingedgebooks.com

CHAPTER ONE

Of course, you've heard of Wenken, Denkyn, and Nodd because they're way up in the six figure income bracket, being oil tycoons out of Houston; and you've heard of Samuel J. Salvato because the old "Corpse," Marine Corps, that is, does not let its better men bloom unnoticed. They're much too valuable later for frightening boots into doing about twice what said boots deem possible or even probable.

Wenken, Denkyn, and Nodd are better known for lesser reasons... or should we say for a less noble reason, since such men are much more numerous than men like Salvato J., Corporal U.S.M.C.R. Serial No. 348-351, simply because there have been hundreds of millionaires, but only one Samuel J.

Me? Hell, I don't count, not when bellied up to millionaires or men like Salvato. I got a kitty stashed away and I won't starve as long as the buck remains worth two bits, but I don't worry Wall Street.

Anyhow, you've now met the principals in this little tale, except such women as became involved, but what say we meet them as they appear. I have known Sam J. for years, known *of* the Eugene Field trio for some time, but the women were met sort of incidental like.

Sam and I were rehashing old times, Saipan, Tarawa, Guadal and such over a haystack of spaghetti, shored up all around by choice sections of a recent fowl, all drowned in a rich gravy at which Mrs. Sam J. excels, when the phone buzzed.

Sam snarled at the instrument for a moment and, when it didn't melt (I still don't know why), and go up in smoke, Sam leaned out, stretched forth an arm a fraction smaller than a tractor tire, lifted the Ameche off the hook, and thundered briefly into the mouthpiece.

"He's here," said Sam, in precise English, "but at the moment he's feeding his face and doesn't desire to be disturbed ... What? Look, buster, I don't give the rind off a hunk of Romano who you are ... Hunh? Oh, you represent them, eh? Well, I am Mr. Barden's executive secretary and you can tell me whatever it is ... Well now, is that a fact ..." Sam scowled uproariously and puffed until he wasn't a bit larger than a prize Hereford bull. "Dew tell ... Wenken, Denkyn, and Nodd ... Okay, tell that bedtime trio that as far as the executive secretary is concerned ... I've just told you. You can't speak to him, and for all of me you can go jump ..." He glared at Sadie because she kept him from really fusing the instrument into a hunk of metal. Sadie has been fending off those glares for so long they don't dent her anymore.

"That's right. You can tell those filthy rich hoodlums that they can ... That's fine!" He crashed the receiver down and grinned at me, showing a mouthful of teeth that had once made gruel of a Jap's thumb.

"Look," I said heatedly, "those men are millionaires, and I make my living nosing into odd places. Maybe one of their daughters has eloped with a chauffeur. Now you've killed it."

"I have striven," replied Sam, waving a hunk of French bread like a saber, "to drill a little wit into that so called skull of yours where you carry what we shall charitably and euphemistically call a brain. Never be anxious in your racket. Make them come begging."

"Well, hell. Maybe they'll get someone else."

"Nunh-unh." He skillfully wound four-hundred and forty yards of spaghetti on his fork and slid it into his mouth, reaping only a single, red freckle on his shirt front ... an area equal to half a billiard table. "Since me'n you got old man De Forest's gal off the hook down at Galveston, you got a name. I got to see that you keep it. Remember now, those smelks are nose deep in Morgenthau mash... or is it Snyder? Well, you can't alliterate with Snyder. They're so rich they're unsanitary."

"Unsavory is the word you want."

"Don't tell me what word I want, but as I was saying, bite them till it hurts. They want you, so they called you... *ergo* it is you they want... *per se... sic semper tyrannis.*"

"*Poo'o faa'a pi fea mai oe,*" I shot back.

Sam started another four-forty and grinned. "My Samoan is a little rusty, son. It's been years."

"To some minds," I sneered. "Thing is, you run a grocery store. That, I suppose, qualifies you to tell me how to run my business."

"Dear boy," he shrugged, titanically, that being the only way he can shrug, "someone must provide the strategy for your tawdry profession." He defted the forkful of spaghetti into his mouth.

"I'm not for hire, anyway," I said. "I work for Uncle."

"Not anymore. You dislike George Marvin intensely and have sent in your resignation."

"How did you know that?" I exploded.

"You told me," he replied, patiently.

I tackled my spaghetti with a will because I have no memory to speak of, and Sam has one like an elephant and, when he gets started, he always manages to come up with some remark that makes my ears burn.

"Gonna spend the night?" he asked, as he mopped up red gravy with bread.

"Guess not. I've got to take a chick to the Shamrock tonight."

"Mercy... nothing but the best, I take it. Is the chick up to my standard?"

"If you mean up to Sadie's standard," I countered slyly, "there ain't no such chick."

"Hah," barked Sadie, her soft brown eyes shining. "Frank told *you*... bub."

"A mere rub off my own brilliance," said Sam, in no way put out by my devastating repartee. "A man cannot associate with brilliance without becoming somewhat sunburned by it. I'm not niggardly."

I Shamrocked the chick, and lost a rather large bet I had made with myself because, once we were out of the place, she developed one of those cases of "I-gotta-work-tomorrow-and-must-get-some-sleep" itis. So home she and I went... separately.

I have a nice little concrete block house way out on Pringle not far from the Gulf Freeway, and it's lonesome by one's self, but it was too late to do anything but go home. I went in (the place still smelled new), tossed my coat on the tan plastic sofa, and went to a built-in wall bar and swung her out. I have bourbon, rye, and scotch for my friends, but a jaunt that carried me to Porto Rico fell me in love with a rum they put out down there called *Donna Angel*. It is smooth as a virgin's breast, wickedly amber, and very light, with a delayed action fuse that calls out its wallops in a custard contralto.

I had fallen out on my couch, comfortable and relaxed, and was listening for the contralto to speak from the heart of the burn three inches below my sternum that was swelling into a feeling of incorrigible well being, when a horn, veddy authoritative and rich, blatted in front of my house. I frowned and sat up. All my friends know that a horn sends stiff, black hairs erect on the nape of my sixteen inch neck when blown demandingly in front of my house, and I have been known to be uncivil about it. Again it blew, and you could almost smell that Cad. I got up and peered through a little Judas window I have in my front door and there, against the curb, reclined... not a Cad, but about twenty-thousand bucks worth of Rolls, its sedate black enamel gleaming richly, and its chromium managing to give the impression that it was sterling. The horn romped again, so I said something very nasty, and turned back to my drinks. After ten minutes of blowing, it stopped, but the car didn't start. Instead, a heavy hand banged on my door hard enough to rattle the windows. By now I was in a state of mind that bordered on the berserk. I threw the door open and said to the thick chauffeur standing on the porch: "There's a doorbell, or isn't your intelligence up to pressing a button?"

The face was oak and didn't move a muscle. The eyes were black hunks of anthracite and as opaque as mud.

"You Frank Barden?"

"What's it to you?"

"Mr. Denkyn wants to see you." His voice had been slugged too many times and it screed on the turns; his ears were great, distorted mushrooms of cartilage grown to the sides of his head.

"What makes you think I give a tinker's damn about what Denkyn wants?"

"Better do this quiet," he said, still as rocky as a cliff. "He says bring you to his home. I'm bringing you."

"Look, you pummel-faced son of a one-eyed Aztec..."

"Come out here and say that."

I did and, coming through the screen door, I managed to send it into him with a crack, but he just swayed back a little and stood there waiting for me. Luckily I had been taught to fight the way you fight for keeps, and you never get over expecting the other guy to do likewise. He did and, instead of his foot getting me where I lived, and ending the fight, I moved aside and caught his heel. That's all it took and down he went, his head cracking hard on the concrete floor. I sat in a swing that had come with the house, and that I hadn't had enough energy to take down, and watched him come to by degrees. He was a dope, because he got up before he was able to navigate and, having a mad on, I tiptoed on him and sent him reeling backward into the yard, where he went into spiritual and physical decline for a good three minutes on the grass of the deck. This time he didn't get up until he had some of the cobwebs swept aft. He parried my left lead without any trouble, but what he didn't know was that the lead wasn't meant to land; instead, it hooked onto his parrying forearm and, in less than a flash, he took a nasty tumble to the deck again. As he landed, he lashed out with a boot and near broke my ankle, for which reason I put a little more vim into my return *savotte* than was either necessary or good tactics. I might have missed, but I didn't, and this bird's face had another Purple Heart to sport. I wiggled my foot experimentally, knowing that this time he wouldn't be getting up so soon. I piled him into the Rolls, went around it, got under the wheel, and drove the car down the street for five blocks, took a look at Bug Ugly, and saw that he was breathing all right.

I shoved the keys in his mouth, left the rabbit foot dangling on his chin, and hoofed it on back home. I managed to get another gill of *Donna Angel* down, then turned in and got a fair, half-night's rest.

Maybe I should say I intended to get half a night's sleep but it was a vain hope. Come seven, or thereabouts, comes more banging on my door. I lurched erect, sitting, of course, and started reeling in my senses, all of which had been scattered to the four winds during the night.

After the last one was hauled back to the mast, screeching with resentment, I stumbled out of the bedroom, about a third of me wrapped in a bathrobe of satin brocade, whose sash ran around like a frightened snake, making me mutter with exasperation. I stopped, made a determined chase, caught both ends, and tied them viciously, pinching my belly painfully in the process. I paused in the living room, thought it might be my recent visitor, went to a table, pulled forth a pair of home-made brass knux, and slid my fingers into their chill embrace. I was tired of this game and was of the mind to break it up permanently. I went to the door and threw it open, backing up a couple of steps to get the range of this small, elegantly contrived *chatte* who stood on the threshold, clad simply in a straight sheath of a dress made of some softly luminous stuff, ice blue. It hugged her softly curved hips with the indicated sort of affection, dipped in where her waist narrowed down to a one-handed span, then punched out dangerously into two exciting, little tents where her breasts fought insurgently against whatever confinement she affected. She had a face that was strong, but still soft and infinitely appealing, with a saucy nose and full, passionate lips. Her eyes were a gentle brown, large and as clear as *Donna Angel*. A naughty nimbus of soft black curls framed the face just the way her face should have been framed.

"Gulppp," I swallowed noisily, snapping unbelieving eyes at her.

"Well," she bit out, "am I to stand here all day and endure your gawking?"

"By no means," I said, retrieving my gallantry so fast it stumbled and fell. "Enter my dismal den and allow me to ply you with coffee, eggs scrambled in Worcestershire, sherry, and thick cream, and saltrising toast. Rashers of bacon will appear like magic."

She smiled, making me hold my robe tight to keep the back of it from flying up like a roller shade. "I'm afraid that would make you resent me when I ask my favor."

"Favors yet! What sort of favor?"

"Please don't accept the offer you had last night."

I caught her by an arm ... the touch made my fingers feel like I had tried to throttle a Model T coil at racing speed ... ushered her into the living room, and seated her in my best green nub overstuffed.

"Now," I said, taking the couch. "Come over that again."

"I asked you not to take the job that was offered you last night."

"I'm Frank Barden. You reciprocate and let's proceed from there."

"I'm Dene Coniver."

I nodded. "Dene Coniver. Now Dene, aside from being better medicine for sleep-drugged eyes than any collyrium I can think of, what or who are you?"

"I'm Thaddeus Denkyn's secretary."

I eyed her carefully for a moment. "Like most women, you like your little mystery…"

"There's no mystery…"

"Let me lay it out for you. Thad Denkyn and his improbable partners, Wenken and Nodd, try to shanghai me into a job. Right there I'm suspicious. A plug is sent here with orders to seat me dead or alive in a fortune on wheels and bring me to heel. I work him over because he has been reared on a diet of block, hook, and counterpunch, and doesn't know the mysteries and practicality of the *savotte,* the chop, and a few other nice unsportsmanlike, but productive tactics. I go home and woo sleep, which is aborted at seven in the morning by Dene Coniver, secretary to the man who wants to hire me. She says I shouldn't do it. Ergo… mystery. Now give."

She folded her hands in her lap, held her knees close together, and shot them into one corner of the chair. She lifted her eyes and cut loose with a few thousand ohms of personality which left me feeling like the time I went to sleep under a mercury vapor lamp at the Y. "I'm asking it as a favor."

"To whom? You already mentioned the favor angle."

"I can't tell you. Please believe me when I say that if you take the job, you'll be bitterly sorry."

"Sorry I've been, as well as disappointed, but I recover fast. I never get bitter."

"Then you'll take it anyway?"

"Of course not. I've refused and I'm still refusing. That's what makes your visit a little strange. Surely you must have known I had refused."

"Then as a favor to me, go on refusing."

Cussit, she had me interested now. "You might make a better showing if you'd tell me what you mean."

Her dress had crept up a little and showed me a tiny triangle of skin above the smoky mist of nylon that lacquered her slim lovely legs. "You'll have to take my word for it."

"I will. So far you have only indicated a desire."

She got up. "I can't tell you any more. Promise me you won't take it."

I got up also, and my six-one topped her by a good bit. I looked down paternally, making me a negative liar. "Honey chile, you ain't making sense. I told you I had refused the job."

"Keep on refusing it ..." She came close, tiptoeing, and kissed me on the lips, enveloping me in a fragrant warmth that was staggering in its impact. "Goodbye, Frank." She was gone. I slanted backward, letting the couch catch me. I had a crazy impression that her dynamism had knocked me into a sitting position.

After a while, her unsecretaryish impact softened, and I managed to get in a little objective thinking about the setup. I had described the situation to her quite well, and I didn't see any sense in pondering over the details I had mentioned. They stood for themselves. I began to get curious because the setup began to send off a slight odor. Dissension in the ranks? Secretary getting a case of conscience due to operations which millionaires have come to think of as "tactics," or other procedures that take millions to make you stomach? I shook my head and went back to the kitchen, where I proceeded to build the breakfast I had advertised in vain. I consumed it, thinking what she had missed ... not to mention what I had missed by seeing her eat. I could see in my minds eye that delightfully smooth triangle of skin that showed briefly. I caressed it with mental hands, almost shocking myself out of an appetite.

As I was washing the dishes, the phone rang and, after waiting the proper length of time, I went out in the little hallway and lifted the receiver. "Start talkin," I barked, giggling as the speaker gulped and recovered from what usually sets 'em back a notch or two.

"Mr. Barden?" It was a man with a smooth, syrupy voice.

"That's correct."

"Good morning, Mr. Barden. I'm Thaddeus Denkyn."

"Is that good?"

He loosed a chuckle. "You're a jester, Mr. Barden, although I doubt that Dicky would think so at the moment."

"And who is Dicky?"

"My chauffeur. I think he's a little put out at the way you handled him."

"Doubtless. I was a little put out at his approach. In fact, I was a little irritated."

"You evidently were respectably enraged. Not many men could handle Dicky in that fashion."

"Not many men are as good as me," I retorted, modestly.

"So we have been led to believe. That's why we are anxious to secure your services."

"Just what would my services be called upon to perform?"

"Couldn't we discuss that at a more propitious time, at a better place?"

"Could be. I'm listening."

"Could you come to my house for lunch?"

I hesitated. I was getting in deeper than I wanted to, but I'm a curious man. "I think I can make it."

"Excellent. I live in River Oaks." He mentioned a street and number that didn't have to register. I knew the place, but I hadn't known that he owned it. An eccentric millionaire who had delusions of all sorts, including one that made him build a fortress instead of a home, once occupied it. He lived in mortal fear that some of the suckers he had fleeced, in his rise from shoe-shine boy in Chicago to oil magnate, were laying for him with blood in their eyes. It was a perfectly square, two-storied pile, which sat in the middle of an acre lot. It was surrounded by a cyclone fence twenty feet high, topped with barbed wire, and a smooth copper cable that carried four and forty-hundred volts. The house proper had all sorts of peepholes, secret passages, burglar alarms, and four machine-gun mounts on the roof. The first owner had, as added insurance, a yard full of man-eating dogs. Just outside the fence, there was a hedge of privet so thick that a rabbit might have quailed at the thought of penetrating it.

He died early, as befits people living with a conscience in deadly fear of assassination, and Thaddeus Denkyn had bought it. He had renovated the place from top to bottom, put porches on the bare block of a building, and had made it quite livable. No one was sure what he had taken out, and what he had left in of the former fixtures, but it was certain that it was still a fortress. The fence remained, as did the thick hedge and, as I drove up, I found that the house couldn't be seen from the street. There was a button on a post where you stopped before entering the grounds, but I found it only warned the house that there were visitors... it didn't open the gate. After a few seconds wait, the staunch iron gates drew back silently and I drove my heap through, followed a winding hedge-bordered driveway for a distance, then came to a stop under a concrete *porte cochere*. I didn't bother to go to the front door, but punched a bell button at the side entrance, where I was met by a girl that set me back harder than Dene had. She was a tall, slim, beautifully-sculptured, Texas corn tassel blonde with that hardy, tan skin that takes age and the elements in stride. Her eyes fairly struck me as she looked down. They were blue and big and hard-headed... you know how eyes can be when they carry a challenge all the time, like an insult. She tried to make her big, full mouth fall into step with the eyes, but it was too lush and inclined to petulance to behave. Her nose was thin, but straight and lovely.

"What is it?" she inquired, running her thumbs into the tops of blue jeans. Above the jeans was six or seven inches of milky tan stomach, where she had tied the tails of her white shirt high under the pouting escarpments of her full breasts.

"I'm Frank Barden," I began, tentatively.

"Who said you weren't?" Her voice was low and husky, just as you expected it to be.

"I haven't had any argument lately," I said, pouring magnetism into a grin which was intended to melt things down a good deal. It worked. She smiled, too.

"I'm Evelyn Denkyn. I'm sorry if I was rude. What do you want?"

"I have a luncheon engagement with your father."

"You would think he'd have told me, wouldn't you?"

"You the cook?"

She smiled, showing deep, attractive dimples and twin rows of sound, white teeth. "No, I don't cook and you'd better be glad. Since mother died, though, I've been a housekeeper of sorts, so I ought to know these things. I'll tell the cook to water the soup."

"Is your father in?"

"Yes ... Say, are you the man who's been pulling the beards of the great? The one who nearly beat Dicky to death?"

I admitted modestly, as is my wont, that I was.

She leaped forward and smacked me hard ... I don't mean she hit me, she kissed me. This was a kissing company, it seemed. She ran her fingers up behind my head and twisted her mouth wetly against mine. I rarely get set back so hard that I can't recover, so my arms went around her and I joined the game with gusto. She wanted to quit, but I wasn't having any quite yet. She fought with surprising strength for a moment, then went lax. Then I put some finesse into the battle, letting my hands wander over the strong cleft in her back, and tasting the pressure of her young breasts on my chest. Her jaws slackened, which was what I wanted and when, a moment or so later, I let her go, she staggered a little, her lips trembling and her eyes three shades darker, almost purple. "Lord," she breathed, shakily, "can't you take a little kiss of appreciation without devouring a girl?"

"I was afraid you might, since we've only met, do less than your best from shyness. I wanted to show you that you needn't be shy with me."

"You did. I'll take you to Dad now."

"One moment. Why does it please you that I romped on Dicky?"

Her eyes clouded. "Because he thinks he's God, and I hate him."

"Why? Isn't he just a servant?"

"I sometimes wonder. When I was just a kid, he came and made Dad give him a job. I say made because I don't think Dad would have done it if there hadn't been some pressure exerted. He used to even try to tell me who to date, and things like that. He paws me when there's no one here, and I think he'd do more if he dared."

I didn't like that. "I think I'll beat his ... him every time I see him. No one paws you but me." I thought for a moment tears would come to her eyes, but she blinked them away and, reaching forward, she squeezed my hand.

"Thanks a lot, Mr. Barden. I think I'm going to like you."

"As for me," I put in, gallantly, "I like you already, and any time you want Dicky's plough cleaned, let me know."

"And you'll do what?"

The girl gasped and whipped around. Dicky stood there, balancing pug-like on the balls of his feet, his anthracite eyes flaming.

"How," I asked, casually, "would you like to wake up with the car keys in your mouth again?"

"That's one for you," he said, woodenly. "Next time it'll be one for me. Get out of here, Evelyn, I want to talk to this ..." He caught her by the arm and almost hurled her through the open door.

I tensed, timed his turn and, when he faced me, he met a whistler that carried every ounce of heft I could cram into my one-hundred and ninety pounds. It was timed, thought out, and carried that whip-like finish that is the difference between a jaw-buster and a push. It cracked against his bulldog kisser like a pistol shot, spinning Dicky around in a complete circle before he fell flat on his ugly map. He didn't move a muscle. I fished in his pocket, found the car keys, and stuck them into his mouth, leaving the rabbit's foot dangling outside.

Evelyn was leaning against the door facing, holding her breath, her eyes wide. She rubbed her arm and went into a gale of laughter that stopped before I had to slap her. "Did he hurt you?" I asked.

"No... Oh Lord, what a punch... what a lovely dream of a punch. What a devastating, skull-cracking, honey of a punch. He never knew what hit him."

"Come on, let's see your father."

Thad Denkyn was over six feet and a regular bull of a man, with broad shoulders, thick neck, and the red, mottled complexion of a man who once worked, but has sunk into the trap of whiskey and rich food that he wasn't accustomed to. He got up and thrust out a hand the size of a gas mask carrier and shook mine. "Glad to meet you, Barden," he said, in his carefully modulated voice. It wouldn't take much to make him roar like the Bull of Bashan.

I murmured politisms and took the leather-covered chair he indicated.

"You met my daughter, I take it?"

"Yes, sir..." My right was dead, as though it had come in contact with high voltage. That had been the punch to end all punches. "She let me in."

"And," chortled Evelyn, still tickled to death, "Dicky shows up, tries to push me out of the room. He is now in the den, his eyes as glassy as marbles with the car keys in his mouth."

"Sorry about that," I mumbled. "That guy riles me."

Thad's eyes were incredulous. "I had assumed that last night's fracas was something of a freak … but this …"

"Why," I asked, flatly, "do you let this man stay in your house, ordering your daughter around like she was some sort of chattel?"

"Please, Mr. Barden. This subject is a painful one. Shall we get along to the business at hand?"

I nodded. "Let's get along, but the more I see of all of this the less I like it. It's too screwy."

"I suppose so …"

A blackamoor bowed at the door, and said in a practiced voice: "Lunch is served." Dene showed as we trooped into a dining room that had no outside connection at all. The former occupant wanted to be sure he wasn't shot through a window as he ate.

Dene nodded in acknowledgment to Thad's presentation, turned to her chair, and sat down. I placed Evelyn, sliding her chair gently forward, then sat beside her.

The soup was a thin consomme as delicious as the buttered croutons that went with it.

"Mr. Barden, as you know, Wenken and Nodd are my associates and, with our large holdings, we have many things come up which call for the services of an investigator. We should like to have you with us on a permanent basis."

"That might not be good. I come high."

"So does any man whose time is valuable. How high?"

"One-hundred fifty smackers a day and *all* expenses."

That cut his breath, even if his hourly wage was considerable in excess of the figure. "See," I said, brightly, "I told you."

"The amount does not bother me," he replied, with a wave of his huge hand. "I just hadn't ever thought of paying that to one man."

"Think how the people feel when they pay you."

He rumbled amusedly deep in his chest. "Then consider yourself hired. I think you're our man."

Dene dropped her spoon with a crash, but picked it up and wiped away the spilled soup without giving us a glance.

This was too quick, and I wished I hadn't allowed it to proceed so swiftly. "Just one thing more," I said, wishing the soup hadn't been ladled out so stingily. "Why is it that, in a city the size of Houston, you pick me out, and why were you so determined to get me?"

"Mr. Barden," said Thad, suavely, "we know what we want and, when we do, we get it."

"I see." I didn't see worth a damn, and the thought struck me as to how he knew I was at Sam's that day. I put it into words.

"Your friendship with Mr. Salvato is not a secret, is it?"

"No, it isn't."

"Very well. Why do you find it strange that we should try to call you there?"

"For a man who professes the need of an investigator, you seem to know an awful lot about people who don't count in your strata."

"Oh," he laughed. "I think I see what you are driving at. It's simple, really. Edmunds De Forest is a minor stockholder in our company. I think he has invested you with occult powers since you and Mr. Salvato pulled his daughter out of that pickle at Galveston."

I nodded. "That explains it, I guess, although the thought of De Forest being a minor anything in anyone's company seems to stretch my conception of him."

"Just one of his investments. By the way, Mr. Barden, could you arrange to stay here?"

"No, I can't. I have my own home and, unless some task makes it mandatory, I prefer to stay there."

Thad squirmed a little. "I had hoped I might induce you to stay here." Evelyn's face fell, too...and I knew then what they were driving at. I looked at the cracked door leading from the dining room to the den and caught the suggestion of a face being withdrawn quickly.

I got up and walked toward the door, throwing a few words over my shoulder, modulating my voice carefully. "I think I know why you're making such a suggestion..." I raised a foot and threw the door open as hard as I could. Dicky was revealed, sprawled on the floor, blood leaking from a nasty cut in his cheek where the latch had gouged him. I slammed the door, walked over to him, and stamped him deliberately in the face, grinding around in a half circle as I did it. Gristle and bone gritted audibly as I did, and Dicky gasped with pain and grabbed me about the legs as I had hoped he'd do. When I fell, I directed my knees into the middle of his stomache and drove the wind from him in a straining grunt. I brought my forearm around in a hard swing and almost drove his Adam's apple through the back of his neck. I got up again and pulled him off the floor, whereupon he hooked me twice in the stomach, but I have a pretty solid gut and he wasn't in the pink what with this and that. I hooked him hard in the short ribs, then sent my right into his jaw again. I wiped off my hands and stepped back just in time to see the servant place breaded lamb chops and mashed potatoes. "Someone was listening," I said, easily. Dene was as pale as death; Evelyn and Thad almost bursting with joy. "What sort of a dizzy setup is this?" I asked myself, as I dug into the lamb chop.

CHAPTER TWO

Salvato, Samuel J., shifted his enormous bulk in a canvas chair, propped his feet on an olive cask, and peeled the lid from a can of kippered herring as casually as I'd open a package of cigarettes. I once thought he ripped tins open, if they gave him any sort of start, to show off, but I had come to realize he just couldn't be bothered to hunt up a key or opener. One of his favorite jokes was to take a can of beer, the kind with a cap like a bottle, and squeeze it until the cap gave up the ghost and sprayed everyone within a radius of thirty feet.

He ladled a fillet of herring into his mouth and smacked delicately. "So you took the job?"

"Right! And I'm drawing down a salary I suggested more as a joke than anything else, but he took me up on it."

"Did it ever occur to you he's in an awful sweat to hire you?"

"All sorts of things have occurred to me, such as that plug ugly Dicky and his possible position in the household, the secretary Dene Coniver, who warned me not to take the job, the way Thad Denkyn lets Dicky maul Evelyn around, and why either of them takes it."

"It might turn out," said Sam, tearing off a hunk of *pumpernickel*, "that the beauteous Dene is right."

"It occurred to me that she did it to make me curious and cinch me taking the job. He claims De Forest sold him on me."

"I must say that you're exhibiting a dearth of acumen in this matter. It would be sad if you were found standing over a corpse with a smoking gun in your hand and, when the police ask why, you deny the whole thing. I just got here and picked up the gun, you'd say."

"Why would they want to frame me?"

"I don't know that they do want to frame you, therefore I wouldn't know why. The thought crossed my mind. The elegant Evelyn intrigues me … tell me more of her."

I shrugged. "Elegant is right. Lush, long-legged blonde who has had her way too much, given to temper with a streak of nymphomania floating just below the surface, unless I mistake much."

"Young, tender, and top class, or twenty-eight, hard, but expensively preserved?"

"Young, tender and, top class … why?"

"I venture to suggest that her warmth is not nymphomania, but merely a well-muscled nature wanting out. I dare say you used every trick in your bag when you clinched with her. Unless she was inhibited, she'd react … but good. I'm afraid I shall have to lecture you on the fine points of psychology."

"What does a herring herder know about psychology?"

"Some of the world's great men, Spinoza, Nietzsche, Santayana, Croce … were not born brilliant. Some followed mean trades. Food is the staff of life, and I derive a certain esthetic joy from trading in it."

"Not to mention eating it," I sneered.

He shrugged mastadonically. "But, of course. How can I conscientiously recommend a viand without caressing it with my own palate? You may curse my lowly profession, if you will, but pray do not impugn the artistry with which I pursue it."

"Apply your artistic powers to my situation. I've been hired at a fantastic salary and I've not been given a single thing to do."

"What was said about your work?"

"Wenken, Denkyn, and Nodd will put their fabulous heads together and come up with something."

"The nature of which has not been disclosed."

"Right."

Salvato dipped up a handful of ripe olives from the cask with a wooden ladle, let them dribble into his palm, and began tossing them in his mouth. "Franklin, as much as the color of mourning offends my princely senses, as much as I deplore the hanging of crepe... horrible stuff, I sense queer twitterings where normally there is only a placid expanse of epidermis whose usual purpose is to cover my vertebrae. As you recall, it was an infallible weather vane during our recent endeavors in the Pacific."

I felt a twitter or two myself... for good reason. As much as he was given to florid speech, he hadn't oversold his epidermal twitterings. They were nothing short of uncanny, as were the olfactory endowments of a couple of Indians with whom we were associated in that weird collection of genius and muscle which we used to call the C.D.D. Detail. Collector of dirty details. "Does it twitter loud?"

"Not raucously, but steadily. I shall have to consult the portents."

"Do so, along with the Oracle, tea leaves, tie droppings, and whatever else you need to consult. Get me the results as fast as you can because I have a feeling I'm going to need 'em."

As it turned out, I wasn't a bad twitterer myself. I drove home slowly, savoring the thought of the fee I had nicked Denkyn for, and the fact that a day had passed and I hadn't done a thing except earn myself a day's pay without doing anything except... That's the way I rambled on, swinging into my driveway automatically. My garage is flanked with some sort of tall, leafy evergreens that the contractor put there to pass Section seven, clause B of the F.H.A. Code, and from them the flashes came. I didn't hear them very well, but there was nothing vague about the line of stars across my windshield. I ducked, let the car buck to a stop in gear, and fell out on the lawn, knocking off my headlights as I did. I heard the bushes rustle and I let off four rounds of Super .38's into the midst of them, but I didn't hear a gurgling scream, so I figured I had missed. I had.

After a hectic fifteen minutes with the next door neighbor about calling cops and what not (he was shut off from me by a hell of a hedge of some sort of briary roses), I went on into the house mad, scared, and unprepared for the fact that I had walked into my living room with the lights on, a small matter I had over-looked until I saw Dene sitting as demure and cute as a two week old Dalmatian itching for some ninny.

"Backfiring?" She tilted a dark, swallow-winged eyebrow at me.

"In a pig's ... Not backfiring, lover. Bullets! Aimed, as well as I could tell, at me, At least I got that impression." I waited for her to get pale or faint or something, until I realized I didn't have that much time.

I went to my little bar and opened a fresh bottle of *Donna Angel*. "Might I erect you a swizzle?"

"Please ... double."

Aha ... so she just *looks* calm. I handed her the tall drink, feeling a victory of sorts.

"And now that the gestures have been taken care of, might I ask the purpose of your visit?"

She glanced at me over the glass as she took her first thirsty swig, her skin glowing fresh and soft in the subdued light. Her hair was as soft as down and shone like it had been burnished. She wore a simple, little dress of dusky red that gave her skin a pink glow, but that was all the dress gave *her*. She gave *it* the elegance of her waspish waist and the rigid pinnacles of her proud breasts. It was cut low at the neck, in a sort of square, and the twin rises that reached full promise beneath the fabric made gongs ring in my head. If I could just get another drink like that into her ... and sort of kid her along about the job ... I was sure she came about that ...

"You told me," she said, taking the glass down, "that you weren't taking the job."

"So I did. At that time, I didn't know I could ram acceptance of robbery down Denkyn's throat."

"Robbery?"

"You heard what he's paying me."

"Oh …" She took another long drink and leaned back on the couch. "Maybe I'd better tell you a story."

"Make it a good one, and I'll listen."

A shadow went over her face. "It is entirely possible that you won't believe me."

"Entirely," I agreed, "but that's a chance you have to take."

"I had a sister once… In fact, maybe I should say I *have* a sister. She's no good."

"Oh come. You don't have to pause for my help. What is good… to you, I mean?"

"I don't consider any woman who accepts an apartment from a man, money, clothes, and a living as any good."

I shrugged. "I'm afraid the matter leaves me cold. She evidently likes it and so does the man, since he continues to put up for her."

"It's not her first."

"Well, if she's taking it as a livelihood, it probably isn't her last."

She fiddled with the glass and drew her legs up, revealing a tasty strip of flesh above the nylon. I almost dropped my glass, so I finished the drink just in case. I got a new carpet.

"Well, I think one man is the cause of her fall."

I gagged. "Look dumplin'! Get along with your story. Never mind the 'falls' and such."

"Well, he taught her things when she wasn't but seventeen."

"That's big enough to be taught things. I understand they learn fast at that age."

"Oh!" She stood up and sloshed the rest of her drink in my face, which was mostly ice. I laughed and wiped it away.

"Go on with the story while I get more ammunition." I took her glass and met her furious eyes as she sat there glaring and biting her lower lip. I thought I'd like to bite it, too, gently and things like that.

I made two more drinks, slinking an extra dollop into hers, handed it to her, and took my chair. "So the nasty man taught the gal things. Go on from there."

She tensed on the side of the couch. "I'm going to get him for that."

"Oh nuts! Look, Dene, why don't you stop being a fool? If this chick likes the life, will getting someone change her? And by getting, I assume you mean something drastic which, in Texas, is against the law ... although with your legs you'd probably get only a couple of years for manslaughter or something." I thought she was going to throw the drink, but she changed her mind and took half of it down at a gulp.

"You think I'm frightfully provincial and ..."

"I think you're a cute little trick who's trying to ride a white horse. A horse that doesn't want to be ridden. Who else is in on this?"

"My brother."

It struck me all of a sudden, and I didn't know whether to laugh or cuss. "*Not* Dicky?"

Tears sprang into her eyes and she bit the lip again. "Yes ... and you brutalized him so."

"Look," I said, mildly. "If Dicky is your brother, then you must know what he'd have done to me if I hadn't slammed him. He's tough and mean. I might as well tell you that any time he crooks a finger at me, he'll get it again. I bruise so ugly and heal so slow. I've managed to come through a lot of scraps in one piece because I start fast and hit hard. This business of standing around and yakking for thirty minutes and letting some gink get in the first lick ain't for me. I'm scary."

"Well, yes, I know how he is, but *really*, he's the kindest thing. He wants to kill Mr. D...." She clapped her hand over her mouth and her eyes went wide. "I ... I ..."

"Sure," I grinned. "So Denkyn's the guy and you're hanging around as his confidential secretary and Dicky's the chauffeur so y'all can get him. Is that why you didn't want me to take the job?"

She nodded through more tears that almost made me arm her up and comfort her. "It's a matter of family pride, but you're wrong if you think that we want to murder him. Dicky wants to, but I won't let him. He's been in some pretty shady places with Mr. Denkyn, and he's found out something that makes Mr. Denkyn take all sorts of back talk from hint. He won't tell me because he thinks you can't trust a woman."

"Can you?"

"Of course you can," she retorted, hotly.

"Like you letting the cat out of the bag a while ago?"

"That was unintentional ... a ... a slip."

"So, as Dicky says, you can't trust a woman. They make slips."

She looked like a whipped spaniel. "Frank, you won't tell on us, will you?"

"Short of murder, I won't. I have no love for Denkyn, even if he is paying me three times what I'm worth for I don't know what, yet. One thing, though. You might tell Dicky you slipped and told me, or that you told me intentionally. I don't want to have to clobber that lug every time I see him. In fact, the next time he looks crosseyed at me, I'm going to split his thick skull. I'm beginning to get my fill of him."

She came and knelt at my feet, her eyes pleading. "I'll make him behave, Frank, I really will, only," and her eyes filled again, "please don't tell on us."

"Revenge means that much, does it?"

She nodded. "More than I can tell you." Straight out of a book, vintage of, say, 1922.

The sight of her there, pleading, helpless sort of, her eyes wet with clear gems of fluid clinging to her glossy black lashes, made the sissy in me do a flip. I took her face between my hands and thumbed the tears from her eyes. The pressure of her against me started thunderation beneath my ribs that should have shaken the house, and don't think she didn't know it. Somehow, she was in my lap then, her lips warm, soft, and faintly salty. Her body was as pliant as a Dumascus blade, with some of the fitting potentialities of its scabbard. When, some eons later, we drew apart to inspect the wonder we had wrought, her eyes were as black as melted onyx and her lips were burnished and trembling. Her respiration was such that momentary vistas of forbidden territory were visible due to the fabric holding its own and allowing her skin to fall away on exhalation. I went back for more of same, visualizing mighty things. My questing hand, half paralyzed from its contacts, did no more than excite greater efforts at fitting me as closely as possible. I heard a tremulous gasp, and felt better about the whole thing.

"Frank..." There was a little note of despair in her voice. "Frank, don't..." She buried her face in my neck and made a funny little keening noise, but the hand on mine did not attempt to stop it. I stopped it, gathered her into a bundle, and sought better surroundings.

She did not resist. Her hands were over her eyes, and her only motion was her shuddering respiration. From then on, things became a little vague. She was a fragrant ball of frantic, objective hunger, of muscular, uninhibited activity and, from a flood of incoherent speech and gesture, I knew she wanted my hand over her mouth, and I obliged. Houses are pretty close together where I live.

It was broad daylight when I awoke. I tried to get from the bed easily so as to get breakfast without awakening her, but she awoke anyway and scrambled after me. I turned and caught her in my arms, standing by the bed, and held her close. Her face didn't come any further than my chest while she was kneeling, but the feel of her in that position was novel.

"Don't go now, Frank."

"Don't you want to eat?"

"No."

She scrambled to her feet and planted such a kiss on my lips that I lost my appetite, too. It was nine o'clock when we sat with the breakfast table between us, forking up sausages and an omelette with a touch of sherry in it for a lift. She was dressed in a white shirt of mine, and what it revealed was better than what it covered. Without restraint, the cups of her breasts were as delightful as some rare porcelain and, now that we were *en rapport* so to speak, she didn't mind that several buttons were missing. I did; it kept taking my mind off my breakfast. After the last cup of coffee, she stood up and stretched, showing me what a stupefying pair of legs she had, then slid into my lap.

"I love you, Frank."

"I wondered when that would come."

"I won't make trouble for you … calling you and things like that. Either you love me, or you don't.

"I'm not possessive."

"Then you're not human. You'll turn out to be a refugee from a TV puppet show."

"You'll see."

"Right now what I see makes me think of better things to do."

She kissed me, skidding about in my lap like a wet poodle. "I was wondering if you would."

The cab took her away at noon. I had a date with Wenken, Denkyn, and Nodd at two. If I hadn't had the appointment, I don't know what we could have agreed would be a good time to part.

When she had gone, I showered, shaved, and donned a powder blue worsted, tan and white shoes, with a crisp white handkerchief springing from my coat pocket. I brushed the glass off the seat of my car, looked disgustedly at the mess of my windshield, and drove off.

CHAPTER THREE

I cruised down Milam until I could see the glaring white brick of the Killen Building, then looked for a place to park. I should have had better sense. I took a lot, eventually, in spite of shuttling back and forth between Milam and Texas for fifteen minutes, looking.

Wenken and Nodd were puffing on cigars and drinking sweet port when I was ushered in. Nodd was a half pint, bent a little, with stringy, mousy-colored hair and a yellow complexion. His eyes were yellow as well as the claw he extended for me to shake. He introduced Wenken, who had roughnecked for years and, though he had a paunch, he was still a man of no mean stature. He didn't get up, didn't offer his hand, and didn't speak. Just sat there and glowered. I glowered back, shoving my hands in my pockets.

"Wet-eared potlikker," he growled, with a voice that had called and salted many a steer, if I was any judge.

"The same to you, you slab-gutted old wino," I shot back, making Nodd flutter placatory gestures with his hands, squeaking something like: "Come come, now, come come."

"Too damned dressed up," roared Wenken, sitting up.

"I'm clean, too," I retorted. "A bath wouldn't hurt you, either, unless that's Nodd I smell."

Wenken slapped his meaty thighs with hands the size of a side saddle, and the windows shook as he laughed. His teeth were the shape and color of mossy, cypress knees and not much smaller.

"Got spunk, ennyhow," he chortled, as he heaved himself out of his chair and offered his hand. I took it, pleased no little that when I shut down on him, he had to shift his grip to even stay in the game. It pleased him, too, because he broke out a bottle of rye that might have come from George Washington's cellar. Ambrosia, that's what. He poured a gill and handed it to me as much as to say: "If I'm a wino, let me see you swallow some of this." I did, and had to fight for consciousness for a while. It went down like a ripe fig, then went off in my guts like a napalm bomb, but I made it alright.

"Denkyn'll be along, bub. Set down and tell me about yourself."

"I'm free, white, and past twenty-one. Got good teeth, no B. O. to speak of, unless I miss the tub for a day. I vote, mostly against people. I like good food. Ham from hogs, lamb from sheep that's been skinned right, and thick steaks from Herefords."

Nodd looked sick, but Wenken looked like he didn't believe it. Finally, he grinned again and chuckled. "You'll do. You ought to meet my daughter. You sound like her."

"She must be an all right babe."

"She's a maverick. Some man ought to throw a brand on her and break her to halter. Beatenist woman I ever seen."

"How?"

He shrugged and sighed gustily. "I didn't play her mother fair on the split. Managed to git too much me into her and not enough class. Her ma had class, son ..." He sat back, made a face with his lips, and was silent for a while.

"Top notch woman. What she ever seen in me I don't know, but she was the best thing ever happened to me. Made me save my money then, when I seen something I wanted, I bought it, and been in clover ever since." He sat up and glared at me. "What we payin' you?"

I told him, watched Nodd flush yellow, and Wenken's jaw fall. "Gawd ... what you sellin', a protection racket?"

"I tried to refuse the job," I pointed out. "In fact, it has been said I still should. I'm happy. If y'all don't want me, all you got to do is say so. If you want a crumb, then get one. If you want the article, you got him, but not for nickels. I don't have your savvy with the dollar. I got to make mine the hard way. That's probably what you make an hour juggling stocks and figures."

Wenken glared a while longer, then sat back. "Well, I guess you got a point."

"It does seem exorbitant, alright," said Nodd, wanting in.

I shrugged. "Denkyn has his mind made up. It's left to you two. Don't put me in the position of selling you a bill of goods, because I don't even know what I'm supposed to do. That hasn't been brought up as yet."

"Come to think of it," put in Wenken, "me neither."

"How jolly. Here I've sold myself to a job and no one seems to know what it is."

" 'Tain't that so much," growled Wenken. "I could think of a dozen things for a likely lad to do in this business. For instance, one of our men turns up last week with a fist full of leases as rich as oil wells. We proved the land wildcatting, and he turns up with some of the juiciest acreage. Claims he's had them five years. If we could prove he didn't no such, we'd have the deadwood on him."

"What could you do? He might have gotten them legal."

"Sure he did, but when?"

"As long as he has them, what difference does it make?"

"Yeah ... but I'd fire the behind off him if he pulled such a trick."

"And he'd still have the leases. Why not get them out of him?"

"How?"

"Where does he operate?"

"He's in Louisiana now, looking over some land on the Gulf Coast."

"Where are these leases you think he bought on his own?"

"Between here and Galveston."

"I thought that land was all spoken for years ago."

"Not this. It's a tremendous plot that's divided up among a big family of guineas, and you know how they are."

"There ought to be a way … Maybe I'll think of something."

"You do, and I'll think you earned your pay a hell of a slice over what we're payin' you … and I'll come across with it."

"Fair enough."

Denkyn walked in, trying to be unctuous and suave … like a bull whose serving days are over. "Well, well, well. Glad to see you've gotten acquainted. What do you think of him, Nodd?"

Before Nodd could clear the jaundice out of his throat, Wenken answered: "He'll do. What'd you have in mind for him?"

"Well, er, just anything that might come up. Over at Wetdome, we've lost a lot of tools and stuff …"

"Horse hockey." Wenken didn't buy that. "We've always lost a few tools and gasoline and cement. The men take that as baksheesh."

"I think it should stop." Denkyn didn't like his partner's tone.

"You goin' hungry? If you is, I'll feed you once a week."

"Don't be stupid, Wenken. There's no reason to pay those men twice."

"You've paid this young feller *three* times, and he ain't done nuthin' yet. If all you got to do is send him on dogs errands, then I'll use him."

"Where?" He came up on his toes a little to ask that question … a little too much so, and I got a twitter of the Salvato variety. He was just a little too anxious to know that one thing.

"What difference does it make?"

I jumped in at this point to keep him from answering the question. "I'll still be around Houston, Mr. Denkyn. He wants me to look into some leases that he thinks belong to the company." Denkyn nodded easily, and sat down.

"Oh yes, that Bramlett business. He's a good man, but sometimes I think he's too good for us."

"Now that," said Wenken, leaning forward, "is a job for a
high paid man...not smellin' around rigs seein' who snaffles a
tankful of gas and such truck."

"Maybe you're right," agreed Denkyn, with a little too much
enthusiasm. "You see, Ed, this man is very capable. I heard about
him from De Forest, and De Forest thinks there's nothing he
can't do. I decided that on account of Bramlett and...well, for
anything like that, he'd be valuable. When we want him, we
don't want to have to search him down. We pay him and keep his
services for ourselves."

Nodd said: "A capital idea Denkyn. I think we'll be glad of
it."

"Some of us will," said Wenken, ominously, something I
didn't get at the time. I got up to leave, and Wenken followed
me out to the corridor. "Son, how'd you like to come out to my
place and get the lay of the land? We might put away some of
them Hereford steaks you was talkin' about. I got the deep freeze
loaded."

"I think that would be a good idea." I liked the old guy, which
made the company bat three-thirty-three with me. "Maybe we'll
have several things to talk over, too."

He winked ponderously. "Y'can bet on it, son. Tell you what,
run out to the Hartwell Airport...that's a few miles toward
Laporte from Pasadena...and tell Dalton Brown to fly you out in
my crate. I live the other side of Austin, twenty or thirty miles. I
come in here two, three days a week on business. He does most
of my flyin', when Marlo ain't in the notion."

"Who's Marlo?"

"My daughter. Funny name ain't it? Wife done that. My middle name's Elmo, and her'n was Margaret. It's a combination. So's
Marlo...damndest combination I ever seen...too much of me,
though...see you." He turned and lumbered back into the office

on a pair of boots that must have made Justin's mouth water when the order came in.

I waited around the ground floor lobby until Denkyn came down. I expected him, because he seemed to be the playboy of the three, and I didn't figure he'd stay around too long. I touched him on the arm, and he jumped a foot off the terrazzo.

"Wow! You scared me."

"You scare easy."

"That's why I didn't want to talk too much in front of them. I might need you."

I didn't ask him to explain, and he didn't offer anything else.

"Who," I asked, casually, "would be glad if I was dead?"

"Why... I'm sure... I have no idea. Why do you ask?"

"I was shot at three times last night in my driveway. Where was Dicky at the time?"

"It could have been him. He took me to Austin last night... Fooled around for some time. At what time were you fired at?"

"It wasn't him if you were in Austin, but someone don't like me. The only new thing I've done in the last few days is agree to work for you. Who knows about it?"

He shrugged. "I don't know... a good many people I guess. I've made no secret of it."

"Forget it. Maybe someone doesn't like the color of my ties."

"You are given to flippancy at odd times, Mr. Barden."

"Don't let it disturb your bowels, pal. I like it that way."

I left him standing there, found my car lot, and handed the attendant my card. He brought the car around, looking through the holes in the windshield. "Somebody don't like you."

"How right you are," I said, as I thumped him a quarter.

I didn't care about going home at the moment. Alright, I was scared to, so I took the Galveston road with Sam Salvato in mind. I wasn't really scared to go home, but last night's experience was pretty clear yet and, though I'd have to take it home sooner or later, right now I felt that later would be an improvement on now.

Sam was in the kitchen singing the "Barcarolle" from "Tales of Hoffmann" in a thundering baritone that made the grass in the yard vibrate. When I walked in, he had a slab of red, smoked ham in his hand and was halfway to his mouth with it. Never being a man who allowed mere people to interfere with eating processes, he took a giant bite out of the slab and waved the remnant at me in a gesture which I took to be an invitation to sit. I did, provided myself with a butcher knife that a cavalryman might have soon tired swinging, and hacked a steak from the ham. Sam purloined the knife, attacked a huge hunk of Romano, and tore off half a loaf of tough, sour Italian bread, handing the rest to me. We chomped appreciatively for a spell, washing our efforts down with a brand of Chianti that might have come over with Columbus, and gleamed gustatory joy at each other.

"Sadie is visiting an indisposed relative," he said, daintily, as soon as he could clear his mouth without gulping, "and at such times I am forced, against the better facets of my instinct, to forage like a marauding Tartar sacking the steppes of the Crimea."

"Does the Crimea have steppes?"

"So I am informed. However, whether it does or not is a matter of less importance than a man of my standing having to forage like a Tartar murzah on the make for moolah."

"Well, I'm on the make for moolah and, at the moment, I'm foraging top hole. By the bye, do you know of a character who deals with oil leases, carrying the noble name of Bramlett?"

To my surprise, he nodded. "Rather…although the nobility of the name Bramlett escapes me. In what way is the name Bramlett superior to the name Salvato?"

"For one thing," I replied, offensively, "most people can spell it. You wouldn't be a member of a guinea family hereabouts whose holdings in land is tremendous, would you?"

"Ignoring the implied insult," he said, comfortably carving a dollar and eighty cent ham steak, "I might point out that, though the holding is enormous, so also is the house of Salvato. Being the youngest and most anemic of a family of fourteen, having eleven uncles and seven aunts alive on my father's side, all of whom are married, having innumerable offspring, you will see that my own parcel of said land might make a fair-sized truck garden. Why are you asking about Bramlett?"

"Did you lease your truck garden to him?"

"For oil only. He came at me with a mineral right contract, at which I sneered with fine disdain, but it appeared that oil was all he was interested in, so we did business, one part of which seemed a little unethical. He wanted the lease back-dated five years, and presented a fifty dollar bonus for my kind cooperation."

"How could he do that and get it done legally? Don't those things have to be notarized and stuff?"

Sam gazed at me with pity. "Assuredly, but it so happens that Bramlett is a notary. What's to prevent his telling a lie to suit himself, and what would be better, since no one could make him swear differently?"

"Oh."

"Of course. Now suppose you tell me why you're interested in him?"

"Seems that in the absence of anything really important to do, I'm to try to find out why he bought the leases for him self, when he was supposed to be gathering them for his alma mammy."

"Aha...intrigue. Well, since he didn't say a word about me keeping my mouth closed...just asked me if I objected to having the leases back-dated...then I'd say you as good as have the leases in your grip."

I nibbled at a hunk of Romano and nodded slowly. "You know, I've seen some screwy deals in my life, but something tells me this 'un'll take all manners of cakes. Wenken despises

Denkyn, and made a very cryptic and ominous remark relative to how many people might *not* be too tickled if I turned over too much fertilizer. If that's so, why do they want me around when it is fairly well known that I can find my way out of the front yard without shooting a back azimuth?"

"Son," began Sam, didactically, "harken to this voice of wisdom. Never ask yourself why people do things. There was once a man who hired a detective to find the murderer of a friend. He was respectably surprised, not to say incensed, when said shamus put the finger on his employer. Question: Why did he hire the nose in the first place? He was doing all right, with a perfect crime under his belt."

"He happened to be the imperfection," I declared, brightly.

"Indubitably...I shall see the day when I'm proud of you...I should live so long...er hummm. There was a woman once, who drew a forty-five and blasted a hole in her husband, through which a pigeon flew three seconds later without wetting a feather. 'I did it because I loved him,' she wailed when, some time and effort later, she was brought before a court of law. The idea of instructing her that such were the ways of evil, and that society frowned severely on women who scragged their ever-loving husbands, no matter how passionately they loved them, was uppermost in the mind of the court. Although I can think of any number of perfectly bona fide reasons why she might choose to ventilate the lug (I smell a couple every day that could do with some ventilation), there is still the question as to why she chose such a bizarre reason for her act. My Sadie, for instance, loves me greatly; till death do us part, in fact. She said so before witnesses. Nevertheless, should she expose me to the lethal end of a gun, I'd be moved to suspect her motive to be other than affection.

"Never wonder why people do things. If you recall Red Beach Two, on our advent to Saipan, there were cowtracks and twenty-millimeter shell holes aplenty for such lice as you, and Puskar, and Sobel, and Hill and the rest, yet there was not a single hole that would hide a *man*."

"Meaning you?"

"Precisely. I was offended and, at the time, I might have considered taking one of you by the stacking swivel and flailing out a hole in the sand, even though the lack of sixteen-inch shell holes couldn't exactly be considered your fault."

"You should have informed the Navy of your bloated circumference. I dare say they would have laced the area with sixteen-inch shell holes."

"I fear you become sarcastic and we drift afield. What will you do?"

"Didn't you tell me once that you had a spot of land that might have gold on it?"

"I did. I didn't say so at the time, but it might also have silver, platinum, U-238, and other valuable minerals. That's why I wouldn't give Bramlett all mineral rights. Why do you ask?"

I shrugged. "Just asking. I thought for a moment that you might be serious about it. When I see Bramlett, I'd like to be armed."

"Armed you will be … unless it requires wit. Always remember, though, you have me to turn to."

"That," I snarled, "is the one saving grace left in this wicked world."

"There are probably others," he declared, with magnificent modesty. "The problem is finding them."

I made certain on the way home that I wasn't followed, stopping a couple of blocks from there to case the place before I committed suicide again by barging into the driveway without reconnaissance. After thirty minutes of gumshoeing that netted nothing, I drove in and put up my car.

I sat in my living room with a tumbler of *Donna Angel* in my fist and contemplated the future. It was so obscured by lush blonde Evelyn Denkyn, that I gave up and concentrated on her.

I was taking certain mental liberties with her person and, since they were mental, I was barring no holds when the phone rang. I cussed, but answered it.

"Mr. Barden?"

"That's me."

"This is Thaddeus Denkyn."

"Okay, shoot."

"Mr. Barden, since the firm is paying your salary, you might be considered company property, but I hired you, you were my idea..."

"My pop don't get any credit?"

"Ha, ha, ha. Very funny... but to proceed. Since the idea was mine, I feel a certain possessiveness, and choose to have you follow my instructions exclusively. The first order will be to drop whatever you have done as regards the matter of Bramlett."

"Well, well, and well," I quoth, brightly. "How come?"

"There are reasons, Mr. Barden."

"So I gather. What'll Wenken think of this?"

"I am hoping that he won't think anything. After all, should you fail to gather the required evidence, he might be disappointed, but he would hardly become difficult."

"I see. Well, it's like this, Mr. Denkyn. My ethics..."

"I think, Mr. Barden," he put in, smoothly, "that, say, an extra hundred a week would take care of whatever fever your crushed ethics might suffer."

I swallowed a yen to commit murder and effervesced gratifyingly into the transmitter. He hung up feeling that he had bought himself a man. What he had really done was to set the capstone on a whole stack of smells that had come to my nose since this freak show started. Since he wanted to buy, I'd sell, although I didn't have to give value received. I could see that friend Denkyn had set himself up for a twist, and I was a twister of no mean intent.

Dalton Brown turned out to be a little man with the shoulders of a champion swimmer. He had dark, wavy hair that seemed to have a mind of its own, and intense, squinty brown eyes.

"Mr. Wenken sent me," I said, shaking hands with him. "He said you'd trot me down to his place in his crate. What is it, that Cessna there?"

Brown let a chuckle shake him. "Nope. He paid a ransom for the job, and keeps calling it a crate. President Truman doesn't fly in a crate like this." He pointed to a sleek, silver A-20 chocked on the apron with its engines ticking over softly. "He said you'd be out. Ready?"

I gulped and nodded. Some crate. Even at a whisper, those engines fairly snorted with power and, as we went through the bomb bay into the cabin, I could see what Brown meant. It was a dream in green leather, buff leather, and red plastic. It'd carry eight, and they'd hardly get the first joke told before they'd have to get out again. Brown soused on the power, and we blew off the earth like a rocket. I sat beside him and saw Houston unreel and slide behind us while getting a smoky suggestion of Austin in the distance before the Shamrock was out of sight.

In less time than it takes to tell it, the University of Texas was sliding under a wing tip and Brown, sensing the finish, tipped her nose down a little and fed in another half-inch of manifold pressure. The air speed indicator went wild, making me catch an involuntary lungful of air.

"You going to land this mad thing in a back pasture?" I asked, a chill assailing me.

"Not on your life. There wouldn't be a cedar left in Texas if I did. You gotta have braking surface. The old man gave the Army a plot of ground during the war to put an auxiliary strip on. They did a good job of it, then gave it back. He even put up a hangar, then built the house right by it."

We dipped more and suddenly flashed over a good, broad spread with barns, windmills, a buff stone ranch house, and plenty of white faces scattered about. He slammed the exbomber in a screaming turn, then slid her off into the pattern, leaving me to unplaster myself off the walls. We slanted down as the wheels, snapping down in place, shook the ship, then kissed the runway with a fierce *scrooch*. We slowed gradually as the hangar loomed up ahead, and Brown swung her tail around and cut the engines.

CHAPTER FOUR

The A-20 gave birth to us, and there was old Wenken, dressed in faded khakis that cost four dollars and fifty cents a suit, and Justins that cost a hundred bux a pair.

"Time for breakfast," he rumbled, and turned away with Brown and me following.

We sat down at a huge table on a concrete side porch and waited while a wizened old man made noises and smells in the kitchen. I had gotten up too early to eat, and felt like I could eat half a cow...and almost got served one. After a cup of coffee that spelled cooking education in Louisiana, the cook brought my plate. There was a rib chop of heavy beef that crowded the hell out of the hash-browned potatoes. Then came a towering plate of hot biscuits, a tin of freshly-opened Longwood cane syrup, and a slab of golden yellow butter.

"Y'in a fix if you like your meat burned all to hell," said Wenken, running a knife effortlessly through the dark brown surface of the meat. A river of red gravy followed his knife, making a river of saliva flood my mouth. Well, I never ate a better piece of meat. I sopped gravy with a biscuit, wallowed the potatoes around in it...practically foundering myself...and washed it all down by draughts of coffee. Wenken burped from way down like a giraffe, so I followed suit.

"That ain't mannerly," he said, mildly.

"Comfortable though, ain't it?" I said, grinning.

"Is so! Never could go along with all that there folderol about eating, 'cept for one thing. Never did think it polite of a man to break wind at the table."

Brown choked on a hunk of meat, and I almost burst with mirth, but the old man was dead serious.

By the time we had finished that herculean breakfast, the sun had about cleared off the front porch, so we went out front and sat in snazzy chrome and plastic chairs.

"Damn dude-sittin' machines," complained Wenken. "Pretty comfortable, though. Marlo bought 'em in Austin. Never sat in nuthin' but hide-bottomed rockers myself. Now, son, been thinkin' 'bout Bramlett?"

"Yes, and I have a little news for you about that."

"Y'is? What is it?"

I sat up and looked him square in the eyes. "Mr. Wenken, what goes on in the firm that's so queer? You know this hiring of me rings false to hell and back."

He bit off a hunk of Days Work and wallowed it about comfortably in his mouth. "Looks like I'm gonna have to admit somethin' got a pretty rank smell, but damn if I can find it. We get along after a fashion, we make money and, up to a year ago, seemed satisfied with what we got. Then gradually ever'body gits tetchous and starts lookin' tight around the mouth. One reason why I didn't stick my finger in your belly, and tell you to git, was because I was hopin' you was a likely lad who might git in there and bust the thing open. Up to now, I ain' got no beef."

"Alright. I'll play it wide open, but if you let them know it, my effectiveness is blotto."

"The left side of me don't know half the time what the right side of me's doin'," he snapped. "Go on."

"Well, the first thing is this: There's something behind it that I don't get. Something, maybe, that'll get me in a peck of trouble. I'm playing it straight with you for two reasons. I like it that way, because you seem the right guy in the firm ... the others give me

Mexican heartburn. Probably my best reason is this: I'm just curious enough to run it down just to see what makes it go, and I'm going to need someone to pull for me. I've picked you as the man. I got a feeling that if I play foursquare with you, you'll play it right back. You learn about people in my racket, or you don't stay there long. I've decided that you're the man...else you'd be in town trying to lay everybody's folks, like Denkyn, instead of out here in the open where you can breathe, watch things grow, and feel a little like God."

I had put myself out to impress, and I made the grade. The old man looked at me through slitted eyes, then he must have made some sort of sign, because the front door opened and a vision floated through. When I say vision, maybe I'm giving an impression that jumped the track, because this gal was none of your fluffs with fluttering lids and a bent neck look. She stood an easy five-seven, and would have tipped a hundred and thirty without being wet. She was as straight as a soldier and as hard as an athlete, but she had curves no athlete would have known how to carry...and she didn't seem to know she had 'em. She stood there in the door, dressed in Levi's and hand-tooled cow shoes with high heels and pointed toes. The Levi's cost three or four bucks, but the silk shirt with all sort of rope-stitched embroidery must have walloped the old man's poke. It fitted with a certain touch that spoke of tailor and pooed the idea of her having ordered it from a catalogue. She was chested up, not softly and daintily like Dene, nor full globes of grapefruit cut in half like Evelyn. Hers were coned, as erect as a new tulip bud, and as solid as muscle. What they did to the front of that shirt should happen to every piece of textile with a soul.

"This here's Frank Barden, Marlo. Frank, my daughter."

I stood up and accepted her hand, and the light from her strong, tanned face. It was turned gently from top materials, but so mobile that you knew it could turn from cotton candy to granite in a flash. Her chin was good, her nose straight and a little thin … like a thoroughbred, softened somewhat by a big, healthy mouth with lips as soft as custard, full, and given to expressive tremulousness.

"It's nice meeting you," she said, easily, her white teeth flashing in a wide-mouthed smile.

"How'dje know it is?" her father wanted to know.

She chuckled in a gentle contralto. "Pop's always after me to read people's character and, when I do, he feels I should explain."

"I'm astin' you," he persisted. "Did you hear what he had to say?"

"I heard every word he said."

"What do you think?"

"I think I was listening to a man who is sitting on a powder keg, is honest enough to realize he can't see the fuse from where he's sitting, and is looking for a place to land."

He turned to me. "If you're so all fired honest, did she hit it?"

"On the nose. On the nose." I repeated it, because the first time sounded like I was at the bottom of a well.

Those keen eyes jabbed at me again, and he sat back. "Foof." He made one puff, then examined me again. "Right now, you don't know what yesterday was. She coulda said you was a jiraff and you'da bleated, 'on the nose,' like a zombie."

I snapped out of the electrified fog she had laid down, and grinned. "I guess you're right, but she put her finger on the spot."

Marlo sat down and crossed her legs. Long, slenderly strong legs with good, hard muscle rippling beneath their roundness; straight, but with breathtaking curvatures. They filled those Levis, but proper.

"Git along with your story. You got other things to spiel."

"Yes. Last night Denkyn called and told me to drop that Bramlett matter."

A dead silence fell; out of it came a splinter of crossed purposes that I sensed, rather than saw. Wenken turned a dull red and, almost involuntarily, I glanced at Marlo. Her face had gone as hard as stone, and her violet eyes were slitted and hot. Her sensitive nose pulled in at the corners, making little white dimples over her upper lip.

"So you hired a snooper to put on Harold, did you?"

The old man regained his balance quickly. "I didn't hire him, Denkyn did. I'm just using him, and if Mr. Lace Drawers Bramlett is all you think, then Frank'll be wasting his time." He turned to me. "I'd just as soon this came out some other way but, since it's done, you might as well know all of it."

"Excuse me," she said. The vision bounced out of her chair and flounced into the house.

I nodded. "Tell me, all of it."

He sighed, sitting back in his chair. "Bramlett went to school with 'er. T.C.U. She quit after the first year 'cause she didn't like to stay away from the ranch, and I got half a notion she thinks I need 'er as a sorta keeper. I give this Bramlett, who was a football player and a no good..."

"Ah, ah," I scolded. "Let's not—"

"I know. You run through Tulane one year at the Sugar Bowl like a dose of croton oil through a widow woman. I seen you, and won thirty five hundred wagon wheels on the game. I didn't say all football players was no good, but Bramlett is. I'll give him this, though, he's a good lease man. Smart, smooth-talking, and a little too good lookin'. I tell Marlo he's rotten, and she thinks I do it because I think she might marry him."

"Which is right, of course."

"Yap, come to think of it!" He sank down in the chair, looking a little whipped. "Marlo's too good a gal for a tramp like him, but what can a man do? I ain't never claimed to be no lily, and I sure can't tell her to look at me, then look at him for contrast."

"There might be a way," I said, gently.

"Like as to how?"

"I've turned up what I need on Bramlett already."

He started, and leaned forward. "You is what?"

"He leased the Salvato tract under his own name, then gave them fifty dollar bonuses to let him back-date them."

His face tightened, then grew hard. "Where'd he get that amount of money?"

"You got a point there. I'll look into it."

"Might be a good idea. When we get him, I want him plastered so good that Marlo can't open her mouth."

"I don't know about that. One sure thing, she's going to look at me like a dose of hemlock."

"Is that bad?"

I squirmed a little. "Somehow, I think it could be. I think your daughter gave me a kind of shock. Whenever a lovely woman shocks me like that, I begin racing ahead toward possible eventualities."

"I'm hoping," he said slowly, "that her good sense'll be enough to snatch her back to reason. Me and you, son, are gonna put the chocks under Mr. Bramlett … good. If she's still so nutty after he's exposed that she can't see what he is, then you don't want her."

"That's right, I don't," I said, with more conviction than I felt … having felt a twitter of sorts having to do with Marlo and the future.

Wenken spat in the grass. "So Denkyn wants you for his boy. Did he offer anything extra?"

"He did, and I accepted. As long as he thinks I'm as crooked as he is, then I'll be a lot freer to operate. I didn't actually promise him anything. I yessed him, and let it go at that. Bribe money spends as good as any, as long as you don't stink it up by working for it."

"Yap, if the fool wants to put it out, take it. I'm guessin' that's where Bramlett got his cash for those leases."

"Think they're in cahoots?"

"Likely. That ain't the first time Denkyn tried a fast one."

There was silence for a while, both of us thinking pretty hard. There didn't seem to be anything else to chew over so, when he asked if I'd like to ride, I grabbed at the offer. I hadn't forked a cayuse (that's *hoch* western), in a long time, and I didn't that day, either. A Mexican stable boy, whose name had been Bernardino until someone went to California and shortened it to Berdoo, brought me an Arabian stepper that Ibn Saud would have been proud to own. He was as white as a snowdrift, with the thin flaring nostrils and slightly concave skull of a son of Achmet the Great. His limbs were as delicately turned as a dancer's, and every noble line spoke of speed and endurance. I guess my eyes must have bugged out, because Wenken chuckled at my elbow.

"Smatter, get you?"

"I'm got. I never saw a piece of horseflesh like that in my life, outside of a painting."

"Ain't nobody ever painted *that*," he said, with the innate reverence of a lover of horses. "Lookit the fire in him. Makes you look to get burned."

The horse was decked out in a honey of a saddle without a lot of doodaddery, silver conchas, tapaderos, and such. The cantle was deeply dished for solid comfort, and the Bull Moose tree was a leg-hugger. I caught the reins short and made a quick mount, gripping hard in case he fishtailed as spirited horses sometimes do. He didn't, but made a rearing change of direction as soon as I was seated, then came down and pranced about in a half circle.

"Better show him some iron," advised Wenken. "That sorta hoss'll run over you if you let him."

I took off across a pasture and thence into scrub cedar and oak. Once out of sight of the house, I let him slip and, after a moment, I wondered if I'd been wise. The first thing he did was to take a low shrub like a bird, clearing it by four feet. From then on, I stayed in the air more than I did in the saddle. Abdulla was a supercharged demon of fire and muscle, running like a mad thing, clearing dry washes like they were drain ditches, leaping low bushes and practically cultivating the landscape. More than once I found myself reaching for leather, but I managed to get him slowed after a while without suffering the ignominy. When at length we had slowed to a comparatively sedate canter, high-backed and sidewinding, I managed to gather myself together and show a little iron. From then on, Abdulla didn't get much rein.

In less than an hour, my tail began to complain, so I turned him about with the idea of heading back, when who should face me but Marlo on a mare who seemed to be Abdulla's sister, except that she was somewhat smaller, a fine sleek grey, so light as to be almost white.

"Mr. Barden, I'd like to talk to you."

"Alright, shoot."

"I think we'd better dismount. Abdulla gets restless if he isn't burning the wind."

"I had received a similar impression," I said, as I dismounted stiffly, letting the reins fall to the ground. Abdulla, who was a gentleman, minced a few steps away and began to crop grass. I caught the mare's reins and gave Marlo a hand, which seemed to surprise her. She let the mare join her lord, then turned her eyes squarely on me.

"Mr. Barden, I'm not good at beating around the bush, so I'll come to the point. Why are you and my father determined to persecute Harold Bramlett?"

"Because," I said, bluntly, "we think he's not worthy of you."

She sneered. "How decent of you."

"Don't misunderstand me, kid," I said, placatingly. "I'm doing a job I was told to do. Bramlett doesn't know it, but he's already on the griddle. He practically stole leases from under the Company's nose, when he had been specifically sent to do the job for the Company. It was done in a very underhanded manner, and I found him out the same day I was put on the job. It was easy."

"Do you honestly believe Harold would do anything unethical?"

I grinned. "I'm sure I don't know. It would appear so."

Her nostrils pinched in again. "You impressed me, Mr. Barden. I'll admit it. Therefore, when I find that you are engaged in this sort of dirt, I'm naturally shocked."

"What happens if it turns out that Bramlett is everything your father thinks he is?"

She tried to make her mouth into a straight, severe line, but it didn't quite come off. Her lips weren't made for severity. "Until it is proved to my satisfaction, I shall not consider what I'd do."

"That isn't smart."

"Why?"

"Because right now, it looks very much like he is guilty. If you refuse to believe until faced with brass-bound evidence, then the shock will not have been anticipated. It might be a blow."

Her eyes studied mine for a moment. "You know, you have a strange touch of kindness ... and logic."

"I don't think," I replied, seriously, "that anyone not pure swine could be unkind to you. Miss Wenken, I think you're probably the most attractive woman I ever saw."

"Thank you." It was an automatic whisper. She wasn't thinking about me and my compliments.

"Then I can't prevail on you to let this thing lie?"

I frowned. Too many people were trying to get me to lay off ... one going to the extreme of trying to shoot me. "You know, you sound like someone who's afraid of what I might find."

"Maybe I am."

"Need I point out the folly of any such attitude?"

"No, I guess not." Her shoulders slumped as she walked to the mare and mounted, before I could help.

"Thanks for talking to me."

"Not at all. I hope this thing doesn't hurt you."

"Why are you concerned about what hurts me?"

"Because you're a lovely woman. Because your father is an old man who wants you to be happy. Because I'm a man who ..."

For some fool reason I felt a little chokified in the throat, and had to stop.

"Yes...go on."

"Never mind," I said, gruffly. "I'm sorry I can't help you."

"Will you promise one thing?"

"If I can."

"Be as easy on him as you can."

"No, I can't promise that. There are some things about the matter that make it necessary for me to play it rough to get results. I can't, at the moment, tell you what they are. I'm a little surprised at you, Miss Wenken. I took you to be a particularly savvy girl who would want at all costs to find out the truth...for your own good if not that of the company."

She sighed and turned away. "Dinner will be at twelve-thirty, Mr. Barden."

After a dinner that consisted of succulent roast beef, tossed salad, baked potatoes, hot biscuits, and icebox ice cream, Brown and I dusted the A-20 off the strip, and unreeled the world as far as Pasadena, where we swooped down and caressed the runway.

We allowed ourselves to be disgorged through the bomb bay and out into the brilliant sunlight of mid-afternoon, where we stood blinking for a moment.

"Who does the Cessna belong to," I asked, making talk. Brown grimaced. "Oh, some guy dropped in the other day. Water in his carburetor. I asked him if he didn't ever drain the thing, just in case, and he looked at me as though *he* should smut *his* mitts draining a carburetor. A few more miles out, he'd have thought it a pretty good idea...if he could have walked away from the crackup."

"What're those rags on the outer edges of the tail surface?"

"I think he's some sort of oil prospector, and he'll duck down over his seismograph crew so they'll know it's him, and send to the nearest strip for him in a jeep...I think that's what those things are. Never liked to tie rags on a plane ever since I blew my nose once and lost my handkerchief in the slip stream, jamming my rudder control. Had to land with stabilizer control."

"Sweaty five minutes?"

He grinned. "That ain't all."

I nodded, and shook his hand. "Thanks for the lift. See you some place, and I'll buy the drinks."

"Sure thing. I'll buy the second round. Say, the old man says anytime you want the plane, holler."

"The hell he did. That's pretty swell of him."

"He's the best. If I ain't around, call me at my home."

"That's a deal. See you."

CHAPTER FIVE

Right on my heels, so close I thought I was being followed, came Nodd, pulling into my driveway right behind me, driven by a kid of eighteen with lank, greasy hair, an air of supreme boredom, and a handshake like a dead mackerel.

"My son Enoch," said Nodd, proudly... for what, I failed to see. I turned Enoch's hand loose in favor of his pa's, and found little improvement.

"Come in, since, I take it, you have something to talk over."

"Er... that is, yes. I do have a little... ha, ha, proposition, ha ha, that might..."

"Ha ha," I put in, brightly.

"Yes..."

We went in, and Enoch plopped on my couch, putting his cruddy feet on it, swooning back like a sultan.

"If you do that at home, do it here by all means," I said, standing over him, throttling an urge to burn the britches off him.

He looked me in the eye. "Sure," he replied, and didn't move. I lost my temper, grabbed him by the arm, and skidded him ten feet across my asbestos tile floor. His head thumped painfully against the wall.

"Now look here," began Nodd, hotly.

"Suppose you look *there*." I pointed to the blobs of dirt on my couch. "If you don't like it, you can lump it straight out of here on your allfours, and take the unmannerly little creep along with you, else I'm likely to kick the tail off him."

"Now, now," soothed Nodd, losing his heat, "now, now."

Enoch, his eyes burning like hot patches, came up slowly. "I'll get you for that, son."

"When," I asked, catching him in the stacking swivel and shaking him till his hair popped. "Now, or later."

"Later," he said, hastily, backing away as I released him. "But certain, son, but certain."

"Enoch has a very bad temper," said Nodd, apologetically.

"That so? Well, it's about time he learns to keep it under wraps. Where'd he get the temper? Same place he got his bad manners?"

"Mr. Barden, I'm afraid you don't appreciate that you're under my employ, and I'm not at all pleased with your attitude."

"Now ain't that a shame. Suppose you try to get me fired."

"That might happen, you know."

"Want to bet?"

He swallowed, and turned a little yellower. "Never mind that. I came here to ask you to do something for me."

"Like what, now that we're off to such a bad start."

"Well, at the moment I'm not certain, but the idea is this: You were retained to do work for the company. There is a rather remarkable reticence on the part of my partners to talk about your duties. Frankly... er, I may be frank, may I not?"

"Oh, sure. Fire away."

"Well, ha ha, facts are, I'm not at all certain that they didn't hire you to investigate me. I'm quite certain that you weren't hired to catch tool thieves, or check on lease buyers."

"What have you done that you want kept quiet?" I asked.

"Well, ha ha, nothing in the way you think, but for some time I have felt that my private life was being investigated ... that I was being watched."

"Doing what?"

Nodd blushed and, beneath his jaundice, it was a startling color. "That is neither here nor there."

I shook my head. "That won't cut it. If there's something you want kept quiet, then how will I know if you don't tell me?"

"His women, son," snarled Enoch, from the other side of the room, "his women. Where's your brain, or shouldn't I ask?"

I bit back a retort, then turned to Nodd. "Look, what you do with your private life is your own business, and Enoch's, apparently. Neither Wenken nor Denkyn will ask anything of me along that line."

A crafty look came over his face. "How do you know?"

"Because I don't do boudoir snooping. And what if they did catch you shacking up with some chick? Is that something Denkyn doesn't do, or Wenken, either, for that matter?"

"Brother, are you dense," said Enoch, with a smirk.

"I guess so." He had given me an idea, though, and I looked closely at Nodd, who had blushed again. "You look pretty yellow and puny for a Casanova."

"Getting warm, nose," said Enoch, "getting warm."

I shrugged. "To each his own. I'm not shocked, and I don't give a damn."

Nodd, after struggling with his breath for a moment, said: "I might want you to do some special work for me."

I held up a hand. "My ethics," I said, loftily. "Since you apparently want me to do it without telling the others about it."

"His ethics," said Enoch, sarcastically, "will, I think, respond to the usual therapy."

"Of course. Well, indeed, Mr. Barden, I expected to provide an honorarium, um, you know. A slight bonus, as it were, in cash, of course, which you will not have to put on your income tax." He winked owlishly. I let several expressions chase around over my face, then looked lugubrious.

"Then it's settled," he said, briskly. "You'll receive an envelope each week containing a fifty dollar bill..."

"Oh no. Those things cause talk. Fives. Used fives."

"Very well, that'll be all right. It starts as of now. He handed me two twenties and a five, making Enoch snicker nastily from his position under a far window.

"Er …" began Nodd, cautiously. "I had thought of asking you to do some work for me regarding…" He stopped, embarrassed.

"You mean on Wenken and Denkyn?"

"Well, yes, as a matter of fact. But since you don't do work like that…"

"Up the honorarium," grated Enoch.

"Shut up, pipsqueak," I told him, "unless you want to go through that window."

"I'll work for you doing anything that seems a bonafide job. I won't snoop on the other members, and that's final."

Nodd shrugged, then dropped his bomb. "If you ever get curious, look into Denkyn's income tax returns… they are quite artistic." With that, he beckoned to Enoch, who snarled like a young possum, and followed him out the front door. I dusted Enoch's foot print off my couch, poured an overblown shot of *Donna Angel,* and mixed some Coke with it, adding a squirt of lime juice. I sat down to chuckle momentarily at three partners, two of whom trusted each other like a snake and a rabbit. Wenken, they seemed to tacitly agree, was on the level, except that Denkyn didn't want the matter of Bramlett probed. After the chuckle, I began to feel a touch of claustrophobia. This thing was building up like cotton out of a gin-stand and, as yet, I had done very little investigating. Seemed like things were clouding up all over; but there was no break in the overcast. I puffed for a moment in indecision, then decided to expose developments to Salvato. Things had a way of clearing up after a talk with him. So I treated my nerves with rum again, and took off for Dickinson.

I found him in his living room with its tapestries of Venetian canals, gondolas, and mustachioed gondoliers screeching love songs to dark-eyed full-chested maidens. Appropriately enough, he was singing *Santa Lucia* in a low voice that still retained enough thunder to shake my tonsils. He was stretched in a big chair with his feet on an ottoman, bare to the waist, and in his hand was a long, thin cylinder that was burning. It was black and, from the smell, something elegant in the smoking line.

"Your chopstick is on fire," I said, sitting opposite him.

"Bravo," he said, casually. "You have disinterred your talent for observation. I got the idea from a Russian I met once. This is a Russian-type cigarette with top grade Havana cigar tobacco, made by a Mexican to my order in San Antonio."

"The paper is made, of course, by a Chinese Jew whose number one son married a Ubangi."

Sam looked pained. "You jest, when you should be tasting the delights of the senses just smelling this aroma."

"Every time I see you, you're tasting delights. You treat your senses like I treat my women."

"I might become offended twice at that. I do not treat my senses like you do your women, which by and large are a scabby bunch..."

"Careful. You may be speaking of the woman I love."

"No, I did not weep nor otherwise exhibit my sympathy for the unfortunate creature. You came with something on your mind, of course."

"Natch." I told him of the various members sicking me on other members, mentioning Wenken's daughter and what a gal she was, and that Wenken was my pick and, as far as I was concerned, my boss.

"That the daughter is well favored has nothing to do, I'm sure, with your attachment to, and choice of Wenken."

"Nothing whatever," I barked...then blushed at my bark.

He flung two thick eyebrows up into his tumbling, black hair, then lowered one very slowly. "Ah...so! I think...never mind. Proceed."

"The one thing I find is that Denkyn doesn't want this lease business pursued, and Nodd wants me to snoop on Denkyn...aside from the fact that Nodd is a little old for playing pinch, and if he wasn't, who'd care ... then Enoch suggests that Nodd neither affirmed nor denied."

"You take my mind from the artistic pursuit of enjoying an after dinner *cigarillo.* What sort of menagerie have you embraced now? Didn't you get enough trying to handle the De Forest offspring?"

I sighed. "The further it goes, the worse it gets. Nodd left me with the suggestion that if I ever got curious, I might look into Denkyn's income tax report. He says it is a work of art."

"Why, what do you know about it?"

"Ever hear of two men in high places scratching each other's back?"

"I guess so."

"The reason I asked is the recent income tax scandals, and a friend Denkyn used to have in the revenue office ... Let me see. New Orleans? Dallas?"

He shrugged. I've forgotten, but I haven't forgotten the name L. Douglas Coniver."

I leaped like I was snake-bitten. "Says what?"

He repeated it, while I tried to slow my mental processes down to a speed that would allow me to count them.

"Does that name ring a bell?"

"I'll say it does. Whatever happened to Coniver?"

"Retired. Lives in Laporte."

"You don't say? I think I'll have to visit him."

"Have care, little man. I grow slothful with age, and loping all over the landscape dragging you out of holes is not my idea of clean fun ... too fatiguing."

"Anyhow, I think I'll duck over and speak to Coniver."

Such was my intention, but upon arriving home about nine, after making reconnaissance, I had hardly taken a sip of *Donna Angel* when a horn blatted at my door with the touch of a woman behind it. I got up and opened the front door, almost in Evelyn Denkyn's face.

"Hi," she chirped, staggering a little.

"Hi. When did you get plastered?"

"All evenin'. Can I come in?"

"Sure, come on in."

She came in. "Can I have a drink?"

"Think you need one?"

"Haven't needed one for some time, but I want one."

"What'll it be?"

"Alcohol." She flopped heavily on the couch, giggling as her dress flew up to expose her round, lovely legs. I tensed involuntarily and went to the bar, where I built her a rum and Coke. I handed it to her, and sat down. "To what do I owe the pleasure of this visit?"

"I've been expecting you to call me and 'stead of that you go see Marlo Wenken."

"I went to see her father. I work for him."

"You don't either. You work for us."

"How did you know I went to the Wenken ranch?"

"I know ever'thing. I wouldn't play it too sharp with my pop."

"You still haven't told me why you came."

"Do I gotta?"

"Yes."

"Well, sir, you make me tingle places. You put ants in my expensive pants, and … well, must I draw you a picture."

"Nope, you make out okay."

Her legs were still insufficiently covered, and her quick hand covered them.

"Look, you're playing in dangerous waters."

"I hope so."

She tilted her glass and took a long, slow drink. While her head was back, I could see that she wore only a thin silk blouse and she hadn't buttoned it very high. She tilted so far back that it taunted and glimmered richly in the dim light.

She put the glass down on the coffee table, hurled her soft hair into disarray, and said: "Y'know what's the matter with me?"

I shook my head. "Not in particular. You've got a mountain in your chest."

"Two mountains," she said, chokingly.

"I said in, not on."

She smiled through a freshet of tears. "That's what I mean, too. Two…inside, and they hurt." With a touch of self-consciousness, she pulled her blouse together, then forgot about it again.

"Too much time, too much money, too natural, and too much heat in my blood. I like men too well."

"And I like women too well. We might become famous."

She leaned forward. "I must not be. I've been here ten minutes, and you haven't kissed me."

I repaired the oversight with considerable gusto and jumped from the chill she started by twisting like an acrobat. She had kicked off her shoes, and her legs glowed a little whiter above their nylon scabbards. She became a panting, ravening snake, all motion, all passion and demand.

The warm scent of *woman* billowed up and suffocated me with a pounding sweetness that made me go a little crazy, too.

I caught her to me hard and bit her around the ears, making her throat rasp with contracting effort. The noise in her throat rose higher.

"Frank…Frank…I'm…don't hurt me…much."

I didn't; but that was too tame, I found out later…much too tame.

Much later I felt like a pair of winter drawers that a couple of puppies had pulled at. Evelyn was asleep, twisted on the bed like a kitten sleeping in the sun. Her palms lay upward on the sheet, pink and healthy, and her face, that had been twisted by passion, was now almost babyish, and as placid as a pool.

I reeled to my feet, thinking as I did so that I must have been drunker than I thought, lurched toward the door while envisioning flagons of cold orange juice, but at the door I stopped and blinked. The light in the living room was still on, and Marlo Wenken stood there, staring at me, her hands clenched at her sides.

I backed up clumsily and slammed the door all in one motion. I slipped into a jacket and came out, closing the door carefully behind me.

"Sorry," I gasped. "I wasn't expecting you."

"That's obvious," she bit out. "Sorry to disturb you."

She had on jeans and a plain, blue chambray shirt. Her hair was done up in a white scarf and, in the dimness, her face had a stark white quality.

"I was about to have some orange juice. Will you join me?"

"No, I won't. I came to tell you that my father is dead. Now I wish I hadn't."

It snapped me awake and tense quicker than her presence had. "Dead … you mean, died …"

"What difference does it make? He's dead, with a thirty-eight slug through his spine."

"Give me ten minutes. How did you come here?"

"I called Dalton. He flew over and flew me back. I'm in his car."

"Ten minutes." I disappeared into the bedroom, tried to wake Evelyn, failed, shucked off my clothes, and took a quick, cold shower. I donned a suit of khakis, put on my Super .38, covered it with a tan corduroy coat, and came back.

"I'll go back with you."

"I've decided I don't want you, Mr. Barden. Goodnight. You can go back to your fun."

I reached out and caught her by the arm. "I'm going, and I don't think you or Brown singly or together can stop me."

She gave in without more ado, and we buzzed out to Pasadena in Brown's car.

Two hours later, I had snooped to my hearts content while the local sheriff sat in a corner and snored. He wasn't a sleuth, and made no bones about it. "He come in a plane and he lef' in a plane. I ain't no good on a case like this. Fer's I'm concerned, it's murder by person or persons unknown. I'll stay the night."

Wenken had been moved to his bedroom and lay on the bed looking very much alive, but he was very dead. No doubt about it. I snooped, but didn't find any buttons, foreign cigarettes, or anything to go on. Dawn was breaking when I decided I might as well take the attitude of the sheriff. I was standing out at the air strip, wondering how the hell a man could land a plane, get out, walk over to a man like Wenken, and shoot him in the back close enough to burn the flesh. I had spoken to the cook, who had been asleep and hadn't heard a thing. I asked how he came to be asleep when it was still daylight, but I remembered that he was up before day, starting breakfast, so I didn't insist on an answer. Marlo had been in Austin buying supplies, and all the cowhands had been at one place or another on the ranch, which is a fair plot of fifty thousand acres.

Sure, they had seen the plane come in, stay fifteen minutes, and leave. What kind? Shrug. One of them silver jobs you see all the time. Any distinguishing characteristics? Well, yair ... red nose. Wonderful! Silver plane with a red nose. Name of Rudolph, no doubt. Two passengers or twenty? Coulda been air one. Fur piece away and not easy to tell.

I sighed, and pulled my coat together. The dawn wind was a little chilly. Berdoo came to call me to breakfast, and I ate well: three eggs, a thick ham steak, biscuits, and coffee. I sat back, stared at the rising sun, and smoked, wondering what next. On impulse I went into the kitchen, where I met a stare of disapproval from the cook. Berdoo sat in a corner behind the giant wood range, sipping coffee.

"Berdoo, were you around when that plane came in?"

"Yes sir." He didn't say *"Si senor."*

"Did you see who got out of it?"

"A large gentleman dressed in riding breeches, tan coat, and cowmen's boots."

"Why haven't you told someone this before?"

He shrugged elaborately, a lot more Latin than his speech, which was better than mine. He got up and inclined his head toward the back door. Safely outside, and far away from any ears, he stopped and faced me, his sloe black eyes twin pots of raw fury. "The old man … he was good. I'm in my third year of veterinary medicine. He sent me to school and gave me a job, summers. Someone killed him. I think I know who."

"Alright, tell me."

"No, sir."

"Why?"

"I want him myself."

"And stretch a rope?"

"What does it matter? To most people, Mexicans are dirt. To Mr. Wenken, I was a man. He took some talk, I know, when he sent me to school. I want the man who killed him. I'll get him. I don't mind the rope. He used to call me, 'son,' just like he did everyone else, men I mean. What is a rope? What is death?"

The kid meant business, I guess.

"About the plane, I don't suppose you noticed the number?"

"No, sir. I noticed where the numbers had been."

"What?"

"They were covered or painted out, I don't know which."

"Tell me what happened, Berdoo. I'd like to catch him, too."

"I was at the corral, and when the plane landed I didn't pay it too much attention. It was a red-nosed Cessna, and there must be a hundred of them around Austin. I saw the man get out and walk to meet Mr. Wenken. They walked to the house shoulder to shoulder. Ten minutes later, I heard the shot, but didn't think too much about it. Someone's always firing guns around here. Then I saw the man running, and I knew something was wrong. The sun was nearly down, but that was when I got a good, or pretty good look at him. The plane wheeled about and was off in less than two minutes after the shot."

"You didn't notice anything in particular about the plane? The wings for instance, were they metal or fabric? That'd give a hint as to the model."

He shook his head. "I thought about that after it had gone. It could have been a 140 or a 170. Too small for a 190." Berdoo frowned, and stirred his coarse hair with one hand. "There was one thing I did notice, but you see that pretty often ... like coon tails on a motorcycle. The rudder braces trailed strings of yellow cloth."

I froze solid for thirty seconds, unstuck my hard-clenched fingers, nodded, and strolled as stiff-legged as Frankenstein back to the house, where I located Brown.

"Did the bird who owned that Cessna get it today ... yesterday I mean?"

He nodded. "Sure. Not long after you left. Drained the spray gun this time, too, with his own lily-white hands."

"How was he dressed?"

"Riding breeches, boots, and a tan, lightweight coat. Why?"

"We just caught a murderer."

He spilled hot coffee down his front and cursed mildly. "How do you know?"

"Berdoo told me. Remember those streamers? That's how he identified the plane, aside from it having a red nose."

He shook his head. "Burned me for nothing. That job didn't have a red nose. It had a green one, with a green trim stripe."

I sat down with a thump, then thought of something. "Berdoo says he was dressed just like you said. That green nose might have been repainted red."

Brown looked dubious. "Could be, I guess ... but hell, people out here wear riding breeches and boots. A lot of 'em do."

"Yeah. I guess you're right, at that. You didn't know the owner of that plane?"

"Never saw him before. We could canvass all the airports, but that'd be a job."

"You're telling me. You don't remember the number?"

He looked blank. "Come to think of it, I don't remember *any* number. I should have been impressed by this. You know, subconsciously it should have registered."

"Would he be riding around without a number?"

"Not likely." He lit a cigarette, angrily. "Can't remember to save my life about that number. What about the time limit?"

"Time? ... Oh! Well, what time did we get in?"

"Two fifty-eight."

"Was that time for him to have repainted the nose and still make it here by sundown?"

"Damn if I know. I don't know the exact mileage. My time in the A-20 wouldn't mean much where that plane is concerned. It might squeeze a hundred and five with an Aeromatic prop. I think he had one, but I'm not sure."

Well, that had us, and there it stayed for a while. I went in and found Marlo sitting dry-eyed in the living room, looking out of a window. It was a light, attractive room with knotty cedar on two walls, mahogony on another, and rough stone toward the front. The furniture was modern and comfortable, but right now it all had a funeral look.

"We're leaving," I said, gently, as I stepped before her. "Is there anything I can do?"

"Yes. You can go home and never come back."

"I'm really sorry about this morning, but off-hand, I don't know what I could have done to avoid it. Was my front door unlocked?" First time I had thought of that.

"Yes. I walked right in because there was a light on, and you didn't answer my knock."

"Please believe, Marlo, I thought a lot of your father in the short time I knew him. I wouldn't have had this happen for the world. I'm going to get the man."

She openly sneered at me. "I rather imagine your days are pretty well taken up, but then, maybe you operate best at night."

"Did I ever claim innocence?" I asked bluntly. "And have I ever asked you if you were?"

She bit her lip. "I'm sorry. I deserved that. After all, you're a hired man."

"And I guess I deserved that," I said, turning and walking away. I signaled Brown on the side porch, and ten minutes later we were climbing into a pink sun that grew as clear as polished brass as we cleared the lower stratas of air.

I got a call from Denkyn about eleven that day, waking me from a sound sleep, which made me as grumpy as all get out.

"Have you seen Evelyn?"

"Did you know that Wenken was murdered yesterday afternoon?" I countered, as brutally as I could.

"What ... ?" It was a faint scream, then there was a thud followed by a short silence.

"I ... I fainted, Barden ... you shouldn't have told me so flat out."

"That was the fastest faint I ever heard of," I said. "What do you know about Wenken's murder?"

"Nothing. At the moment, I'm a little concerned about Evelyn. She left here last night, looking for adventure, as she called it, and I thought you might be it."

"She isn't back?"

"No."

"Well, she was here for a while last night. I went out to Wenken's place about three this morning."

"Have they made any progress with the investigation?"

"Plenty."

"Is that a fact? Who do they think did it?"

"I know who did it, Denkyn."

He was silent for a while, then he said: "Would you sort of scout around and see if you can locate Evelyn? This isn't like her to stay gone like this."

"Sure," I said, without having the slightest intention of so doing.

"I'll appreciate that. By the way, why did you go out to Wenken's house yesterday?"

"Because he asked me."

"What did he want?"

"He wanted to talk about those leases."

"What did you tell him?"

"What difference does it make now?"

"None, I suppose. Do you consider it your duty, as a citizen, to see that the murderer is brought to justice?"

"How would you feel?"

"Yes, I see what you mean. In that case, I urge you to devote your entire efforts to finding the culprit. Leave no stone unturned."

"I had already decided that. If I see Evelyn, I'll send her home."

I hung up and tried to sleep again, but couldn't, so I glared out of the door at a sleek, blue Buick that hadn't been there when I had gotten out of bed. I gawked at it for a while, then I turned back to the bedroom. Suddenly, I stopped hard. She was standing there, leaning against the door, facing me with a long bath towel held coyly up to her chin. "I thought you'd never finish," she said. "Bring a bottle and some Cokes with you. I need a drink."

I collected myself, springing a dizzy doing it, and hastened to do her bidding. "Where have you been? That was your father asking."

"Me? I've been riding. I woke up at eight this morning, found that I'd been deserted, and got mad. I got breakfast at Beaumont, then rode to Orange, from there to Port Arthur, then back here. You were talking when I got to the door, so I slipped in."

I looked at her as she sat on the bed, innocent as a four year old. "I'll say you did. Think of me on the ride?"

"All the way." She hugged herself, and shivered. She drained the drink, and asked for another.

"Isn't that pretty fast?"

"I'm a fast woman."

I sat beside her, and the touch of her almost electrocuted me. She felt me start, put her glass on the night table, and lay back, slowly stretching like a caged leopard. She was long and soft and wonderful, a mound of joy that became taut and responsive to the touch. Then her arms grew hard about me; her body becoming restless as the sound of primitive passion rose to a song in her throat.

Later, she leaned back, hair spread out in silken masses.

"Do you know that Dene is a little bitch?"

"Evelyn," I warned, *"please."*

"I'll say it again. She's a—"

"In what way?" I interrupted.

"Well…" She stopped and frowned. "I spied on her and Pop once. There. That proves it."

That settled it as far as she was concerned, even though she could suggest no significant difference between her own dalliances, and those of Dene's.

"Don't you think it's time you went home?" I suggested, weakly.

She smiled. "Make me another drink, Frank."

I made two, and first thing you know, I was her prey, and she was a coiled cobra, her mouth a sweet pot of honey. She was warm and strong and the answer to every man's dream. No, I didn't want her to go home, then.

CHAPTER SIX

It was nearly dark when she did, finally. I showered, shaved, and sat in the living room in my shorts, feeling whipped and hungry. I forced myself out of the semi-coma, and dressed. I whirled down the Galveston highway without knowing where I was going, when an eatery loomed up in front of me. I had been there before, and I knew that a finer steak couldn't be had anywhere. So I ducked in, found myself a corner booth, and was soon hovered over by an improbable blonde with chests that would have qualified her for anything.

She was pretty, and had a ton of animal attraction. I grinned at her, and she grinned at me, and we grinned individually, and collectively. In spite of my day of exercise, I felt the goosing of my blood pressure and a suspicious tightness about my neck and ears.

"You sure react nice," she gurgled. "I've been asked three times tonight when I got off, and I didn't tell any of them eight o'clock."

"What did you tell 'em?"

"I didn't. Better order, I can't talk long."

"When do you get off?"

"Eight, like I said."

"Where do you live?"

"Pasadena."

"Fur piece, isn't it?"

"Not too far, and the boss sends me home when I don't get a way."

"Which is usual?"

"Not for me. I'm choosy."

"Gee, you make me feel proud."

"You should." She straightened up, showing proudly why her uniform went in at the waist. The belt forced it. She had 'em, and she was proud of 'em.

"I'll take the double-cut filet, rare, and tell the chef to double the bacon."

"That'll be extra."

"So what?"

"Okay. Want a salad?"

"Yeah. The wop special, and tell the chef to double the anchovies and be sure to use anchovy oil on the salad ... and I know it'll cost extra."

"Drink?"

"Bring me a bottle of rum. You wouldn't have *Donna Angel,* would you?"

"I doubt it. We got Bacardi, Ron Rico ..."

"Either will do. Does Rhino still make those hard, sour rolls that need stretchers to break?"

"Sure. That's a specialty."

"Okay. Specialize me a double order."

"Geeze, but you must be hungry."

"I'll need it, I'm thinkin'."

"You taking me home?"

"Sure."

"Then you'll need it."

She had told the truth, as I could see when she walked briskly away, her full-fleshed hips swaying gracefully, and her round arms swinging in tempo. Great hunk of woman with a pretty face, good teeth, and careful about her person. I could tell! I sat back and munched crackers until she came with my bottle of rum, a zombie glass, and a Coke on the side. I mixed me a cooler and tasted it with sensuous relish. By the time the salad came, I had to have more crackers because I had eaten all of mine.

Then the steak came, as thick as an elephant's foot, almost black on the outside, with tasty bacon curled tightly around the middle. She had thoughtfully doubled the hashed brown potatoes, and I was ready to go. The knife slid through that hunk of steak like you love to see, bringing out rich juices from the succulent lean. Heaven, brother, pure heaven.

I mopped up the last of my gravy with a hard roll and sat back, munching slowly. It had been almost too much, but I managed it.

The waitress came back with the check, leaned over, and I could see the full, exciting globes below the neck of her dress; white, soft, and almost pulled together by her bra. "One of the others don't like it because I'm going home with you."

"How sad. Which one is he?"

"The one at the table by himself."

I didn't look then, but while I was sipping a cup of coffee, I glanced in his direction, catching his eyes. I stared him down, and saw in the process that he was a little drunk.

I felt a tingle go down my spine. He had on riding breeches and boots, but this time his coat was dark brown. So what? Maybe he had two coats. I got up and sauntered over to his table.

"Greetings," I said, lightly.

"Blow!"

I looked carefully at his fingernails, pants, and the toes of his boxed boots. Not a spot of red paint.

"You do a good, careful job."

"What?"

"When you paint a Cessna's nose from green to red."

"How would you like your teeth chipped?"

"By you? That's right funny, Mister. Any time you want to try."

I walked away feeling a little funny and foolish. That had been a dumb stunt. Suppose he was the guy? That was no way to get anything done, except maybe a knot on my head when I wasn't looking, or worse.

I looked at my watch and, as it was only seven-thirty, I tackled another triple rum. My steak was sitting well, and the first buzz was still alingering. I sat there and wondered what species of dog I'd most resemble, what with my day's past endeavors and those projected at the moment. It made me think of something I heard Sam Salvato tell a guy once: "What the hell are you blubbering about? No one made you perform, you know."

No one was forcing me, so it must be me. Good or bad? I shrugged. None of the ladies had any beef so far, and if I was springing a crop of moral traumas, it had been a long time coming... reminding me of another Salvatoism. "The gods were on the ball when they invented close communion between man and woman."

"Then they shouldn't have made it a sin."

"They didn't. Paul did. He wasn't all there." Sam rolled his eyes solemnly. " 'This joy thou hast given us ... take it not away.' "

"You sounded flip and respectful at the same time."

"The flip part was your interpretation ... the respect was in spades."

I glanced at the guy across the room, and caught him glaring at me with a peculiar light in his eyes that I didn't like. I made silly again by going to his table. "See something you want, Mac?"

"I'll let you know," he grated, viciously.

"Do that. Maybe some night you'll be lucky, too."

"Yeah, that's right."

I dawdled along, downing a couple of more triples until eight o'clock, when the blonde made for the car dressed in a cool summer print that seemed in trouble in front and around the hips ... as could be expected, what with the dimensions it had to contend with.

Her husky legs were bare, and her feet encased in flat-heeled, ox-blood moccasins. She tilted her head and gave me the eye, whereupon I stuck the bottle in my coat pocket and tagged along behind. She caught my arm as I came out of the door, hugged herself close, and giggled. "What's funny?" I asked, a little suspiciously.

"Nothing. I just feel good inside. I like you. I don't see many guys I like."

I could feel the warm spots where she touched like ballooning swellings, hypersensitive and delicious.

"Who was that guy back there?"

She jerked away and screamed: "Look out!"

Like a flash I ducked, or so I thought. Later, I learned that I had intended to, but something exploded, a flame of agony sweeping over my head. Faintly, I heard a couple of crisp, sharp explosions, the rapid crunch of feet in the gravel, then I fell headlong down a dark well with cotton batting at the bottom.

I came to on a swank, leather couch with my head wrapped in a cloth of some kind, and heard a coarse, mean voice say: "This is the limit. I told you time and again I didn't allow no tramps in this joint."

I sat up dizzily, and felt the towel turban on my head. "I'll show you who's a tramp," I said, muzzily, "as soon as I get my wind."

He was thick and gross, with a platoon of chins graduated from chest to jaw. His hair was greasy, falling across a pitted forehead, and his face was that of some sort of animal, like a cross between a pit bull and an ant eater. He sported a long needle nose that looked funny as hell on the flat plain of his face.

"I wasn't talkin' to you, crum, but you'll do, too."

My head cleared up suddenly. "What's that?"

"I was talkin' to this hasher here, this two-bit chippy with a wiggle in her seat and a pants full of ants for anything that shaves."

The girl was scared and mad at the same time, but she kept her lip buttoned, and I liked that. She wasn't taking on any more responsibilities for me, so I started a few for myself. I got up and leaned over his desk. "What did you call her?"

"You heard me. You got eyes ain't you?"

"Who're you?"

"What's it to you, crum?"

I hit him a back hand as hard as I could which, but for one thing, might not have done much except make him mad. I wear a Marine Corps ring that weighs plenty, and it opened the meat head above his eye for an inch … and deep. He swayed back, his eyes snapping, and made a dive for the desk drawer. He got his hand in, but so far as I know, he never got it out. Blondie made a lunge for the desk, lammed a thick, hard thigh into the drawer, and I could hear the bones grind as it slammed shut on his hand. He bellowed like a wounded bull, which blondie shut off in a hurry by lamming him over the persimmon with a handy water carafe. He slumped down and gradually skidded onto the floor like cold syrup being poured from a pitcher, his hand still fastened in the drawer.

"Good work there, hefty," I said, admiringly.

"Let's beat it, Joe. This place's got a few bouncers scattered around."

"Why?"

"Gambling in the back and upstairs. See that switchboard there?"

"Yeah."

"Each button brings a different one down."

This was my foolish night, alright, but now I was as sore as one of those things. I reached up and punched one.

"Say, you crazy?"

"Like a loon." I felt for my gun, and she thrust it into my hand.

"It fell out when you went down on the parking lot. I smoked at the bird, but I think I missed him. Nobody who was hit could run that fast."

I leaned over and kissed her hard. "Gal, you're all right. Why'd you smoke him, though? Whydn't you just throw it in his face?"

"Because he was swinging at you for keeps. He wasn't just after peeling you. He had done that already, but he wanted more."

The door opened, and a thick-shouldered lad with a child's face and agate eyes came in.

"Who...?"

"The boss," I said, pointing.

"Well..." He leaned over, spotted the lump and trickling blood on the man's head, and whirled right into a whistler. It cracked solidly, and Number One folded up and buttered on the shiny floor with a thump. I punched two buttons, feeling like a million, equal to at least two... fool that I was. I took a long pull out of my bottle, and put it back into my coat. The chick fumbled with Number One, and came up with a sap loaded with steel balls out of a bicycle wheel. She handed it to me, and I patted my palm experimentally with it, wondering how many skulls the thing had cracked.

Number Two put his head in the door only to have the blonde slam it expertly on his neck. She held him there, while I conked him in a manner calculated to enforce sleep. As he fell forward, she opened the door and there, on the threshold, was the biggest man I ever saw. He was bigger than Sam Salvato, and when they get that big, they're freaks. This one had a better opinion of his three hundred-odd pounds than was absolutely necessary, or safe.

"Hey, there, what's goin' on?" He sounded like a precocious ten year old. He lunged across his friend, catching me somewhat by surprise, since I half-expected him to run elsewhere. Instead, I blinked to the fact that here he was in my face, practically, and he had one of those homemade saps, which he was swinging in an arc, clutched in a hand as big as a Samoan pineapple. I don't guess I ever clipped a guy any faster or harder in my life, because he startled me with his unexpected charge, and I had to hit him clean. My stomach took a roll at the sound of the impact. I could see the whole side of his jaw cave in, as a jaw should that is trying to withstand half a pound of steel balls wrapped in cowhide.

He landed like a dead fish on a dock smack atop Number One, and now there were three. Blondie laughed aloud. "Two to go!" she bellowed, and damn if she didn't push the last two buttons and slink back to her side of the door. "Brother, are you ever poison. This is getting better and better. I was fired anyway, so…" She stopped, disengaged the sap from Man Mountain, and tapped Big Greasy a solid thump on the crumpet just as he wavered up over the table. He slid back and repoured himself onto the floor, his hand still limply pinioned in the desk drawer. She had sent out the five star alarm (or they were getting worried), because the last two, a small, tightly-knit redhead, and a lanky bird with no chin and a lot of bright yellow hair, burst into the room and had the door slammed behind their backs before they knew what happened. Blondie reached for the smaller one, but he was too quick. He snatched the sap out of her hands and struck her a glancing blow on the head, sending her reeling against a wall. Oh, brother! I sailed into yellow hair and missed clean with the billy. I threw it away, not being familiar with it, and drove a knee into his belly while taking his own truncheon on a shoulder, feeling it go dead like a switch had been thrown. He bent over, gasping, and I jacked him up with a right, bent him over again with a knee to the guts, and took a flying tackle at the other, who was all set and drawn back for a *coup de grace* on Blondie, who was still standing but dazed. I struck him between the shoulder blades and nearly rammed him through the wall, but I knew I had my hands full. He was as hard as a knot and as slippery as whalebone as I found out by discovering that I was on the floor and he wasn't. He won the fight for me, because he had been to the movies, and not where you fight for keeps. He had a sap, but I guess he was scared (like me), and lost his head, because he landed on my back, tried to balance himself to take a swipe at me, but found himself in a similar position just ahead of me. I can be a mean one when I want to. I went for him as fast as I could, but I wasn't quite fast enough; he bounced his weapon off the ridge above my eye, blinding me for a moment. I took a split second to wonder what was happening to Thin Shanks, then clubbed my man desperately at the base of his skull, feeling him go limp like a fainting woman. Without waiting to see what was happening behind me, I rolled off and came to my feet.

The gal was wielding the sap this time, with Number One and the slim guy, after two lusty swings, kissing carpet level.

"Any more?" I panted. "If there are, let's catch wind."

"Yeah, out of here, as fast as we can."

This time I had had all the mad knocked out of me and, sweeping the damp towel off the couch, we lammed ... but not before she had taken the keys from Fatso, wrecked the communication and buzzer system, and uprooted the phone.

"That'll keep 'em a while," she said, locking up our opponents. "That place is bustproof, as well as soundproof. Someone'll find them eventually."

"Honeychile," I chortled, as we hit the gravel, "remind me to take you with me when I need the right sort of help. I had you figured for pleasure and softness."

Her eyes glowed in the neon blaze. "And *you!* What a fool! What a man! I got pleasure potentialities, too, if you're not too beat up."

"You're not just talking, are you honey?"

"Should I?"

"Unh unh!"

"Okay, I don't. I may be a strumpet, but I'm a good kid. I don't pick wrong."

"I think you're a liar, too. I don't even think you pick often."

"You don't think it, you hope it. You're right though, I don't pick often, because the pickings on my yardstick are few and far between."

"And in the meantime?"

"There're some I can depend on. I'm not a manless woman, honey. Don't get me wrong. It takes a lot of man for Prett."

"Prett?"

"Nope. Mamma named me Pretty, and I haven't been pretty since I left one hundred and twenty pounds behind, so now I'm Prett. Prett?"

"Very prett."

I opened the door to my heap, and helped her in. She caught my hand and squeezed my fingers. "Say, you're big. I've been honest with you, and you treat me like a lady."

"Far's I'm concerned, you are a lady. My definition runs deeper than a few gestures."

I walked around the car and, by the time I got in, I was seeing a whole spray of things that spread out like a woman's fan. I reeled into the car and slid over. "Get out, lady, and see if you can pilot this heap."

"Best you ever saw."

I leaned back, fought off a bulge of nausea from my belt-line, and made a few mops at the blood on my face and head. I was a mess, and didn't care.

Prett whirled the Mercury out of the lot and sent it sailing out into traffic like an old hand, at which exhibition of smoothness I leaned back and let the cool night wind beat me in the face. She handled the car like a veteran. Had she handled it differently, I'd have told her to park it until my eyes stopped acting like a TV set on the blink. A bad woman driver is the end.

"You live alone?" I asked.

"No. We have an apartment, but each girl has a bedroom to herself, and we don't snoop. If you've got a better place, let's go there."

"I have a whole house to myself, although what with all the excitement I've been having lately, it's beginning to look like the Union station. Say, did you know who that bird was tonight?"

"Which one? I seem to remember a flock."

"The one who wanted you to go home with him; the one who sapped me first."

"Oh, him… Bartlett, Barlett, Bramlett… something… you seen a ghost?"

I snapped up in the seat so fast, my head swam around in a tight circle, and my eyes sort of spread out, like eggs in a hot skillet. "No, no ghost. I might as well tell you, I'm in a sort of funny case. Investigating some of the peculiar wrinkles in an oil company. All sorts of dippy angles keep cropping up, and I ain't as smart as Nero Wolfe. Bramlett has me tagged now, and I've lost whatever advantage I enjoyed because of anonymity."

"Anonymity. Boy, you use the English."

"I learned a few things." I leaned back again and closed the lids over my aching eyeballs. "You know what?"

"No, what?"

"I like you."

"Why?"

"I haven't discovered the answer yet, but I will."

She laughed softly. "I know. I think like a man, and make love like a woman."

I grinned, and opened my eyes. "Damn if you don't take a stack of cakes." I reached over and touched her on a firm, magnificent thigh, a thing of the purest and best. It was warm to my touch, sending a tingle up my arm and down into my stomach that was almost a cramp.

"Turn left at the next block, then count four more, and turn right."

Something made her exhale a pent up lungful of air as she spun easily around a mean corner, checking speed just enough to flash a glance both ways to see if the way was clear; then she sat back and shivered a little.

"If you don't keep that hand within bounds, we'll turn over."

I desisted, and touched my hand to my face. It was warm, and smelled faintly of some ghosty fragrance.

"How can you work all day and smell so good?"

"Because I'm a clean woman. However, after today's work, and that gym class, I feel sticky. I hope you have a shower."

"Shower and tub. Take your choice."

"Shower, this time. I don't think I could wait for a tub to fill." She reached over and tapped me experimentally, and chuckled. "You, either."

I skidded over close as she slowed the car down to a crawl. "There's something delicious about dalliance in a car," I said.

"That's right, except you've been doing all the dalliance."

"Well, I dally, so you can, too."

She did, and I know that if I had been driving, I'd have wrecked right then and there. She drove up the driveway I indicated, frowning as she braked down. "You have company?"

I shook my head. "I doubt it. No cars. I seem to have acquired the habit of going to sleep with the lights on and the doors open lately."

I helped her out, following the gentleman routine again, and we locked arms walking up the concrete.

"Maybe," she said, as I opened the screen door, "you find it a good habit, depending on who comes in on you … Jeepers!"

CHAPTER SEVEN

had opened the door and she walked in, stopping short just inside. I looked over her shoulders and saw why she jeepered so forcibly. There, stretched on the couch, was Evelyn, smoking a long fag stuck in a green holder a foot long. Standing in front of her, dressed in an ivory shantung suit, with a scarlet blouse, stood Dene, her face pale, and her eyes boiling mad.

"As I said," continued Prett, calmly, "you must have had reason for the habit. A harem, I'd call it."

"Nobody asked you, you synthetic, overbloated frog," said Evelyn, sitting up. "Where'd you pick up the tramp, Frank?"

"The same place he usually gets them, I suppose," said Dene, her voice barely under control.

"The same place he got you?" said Prett, calmly.

"Or you, dearie," said Evelyn to Dene, smiling like a cat. "A squirt like you, I can handle; but big bosoms, like this trull here, are dangerous. Inner-spring mattresses, if you follow me."

"I did," said Dene, "and look what I find when I get here."

"Now that you've found it, why don't you trail off home and sleep with Dad, you common, little nasty … or that deformed brother of yours, who probably taught you at an early age."

Dene almost fainted at that, but she managed to stay upright. "Just for that, I could kill you," she blazed. "As for Frank and me, we're in love."

"Hold it!" I gasped, sitting on a handy ottoman, stealing a glance at Prett, who was watching with half-amused eyes. The other half wasn't amused.

Reaching forward, Prett grabbed a handful of Evelyn's metallic hair and snatched her bodily to a sitting position, then proceeded to slap her crosseyed. Once…twice…three times, and each time Evelyn's head snapped to one side like she had been coshed. Prett straightened up and faced Dene.

"Beat it, half pint, before I skin you naked and show up your falsies." Dene, who was now a badly frightened girl, turned with a muffled bleat of terror and disappeared with banging of doors.

Evelyn, cold sober now, reeled up off the couch and took a flying leap at Prett, who did a fade like a professional, and dumped Evelyn, nose first, onto a throw rug, which was a happy thing, taking, as it did, some of the bump. She got up, weaving a little, and met a full-armed swing from Prett that landed just under her ear, cartwheeling her to the wall where, bouncing off, she smacked into another swing that had her left eye moused before she hit the floor.

"Get out, baby," said Prett, in such a cool voice that she startled me. She still wasn't exactly mad; she (as she said later), was in a hurry, and Evelyn was an offnote in her plans.

I rather think the vanquished broke any number of records getting out, but she wouldn't have copped any beauty honors. She was furious, yet scared, disheveled with Irish pennants dangling here and there…not a pretty sight, considering the mouse that nearly had her eye closed. At the door, she stopped and looked a lot of mad at me out of her good eye. "Alright, Casanova, this finishes you and me, so don't be expecting me."

"He wasn't," said Prett, taking off her shoes suggestively, "and now that he has me, he won't be able to use you any more."

Evelyn looked one-eyed murder, and disappeared through the door. A block away, we heard an agonized motor gunned, and tires burning the asphalt.

Prett came into my arms as I sat on the ottoman, and lived up to expectations. We breathed. The next time, and from there on out, she surpassed them. Her hair, though drugstore, was soft, heavy, and fragrant; her body was divinity...and so much of it, with a mind of its own.

"I've...got to take a...shower, Frank."

I held her tight, watching with animal gusto the soft distortion of her against my chest. I felt myself going mad. "The heck with it," I muttered. "Later."

Her mouth was avid and eager again, and her tongue was an exciting javelin. Exploration wrung a stifled groan from her, and her urgings were unmistakable.

I lay stretched on the couch that had, in some manner, been flattened as though ready to be made up for the night, and listened to the muffled roar of the shower turned on full force. I was sore, I ached, I was beat, and the wounds were seeping again. On the throw rug, there were several splotches of gore, but I managed enough gumption to towel my head before I dripped any on the couch. All of a sudden, I wanted a shower, too.

"I guess we should move," she said, disinterring her lips from mine, long after I had showered and rested.

Then, after I poured a drink that would have staggered an elephant (at her specific request), and duplicated it for myself, I sat on the couch and relaxed, dabbing at the seeping blood that insisted on running down my face and the back of my head. In the bedroom, I could hear Prett bustling about with the sheets, making the bed, since any fool could see that it was a mess.

She came out, grinning and holding up a sheet for me to view. It made me blush, and that made her roar with contralto laughter.

I swallowed my confusion, chasing it with a drink, and shrugged the whole matter into limbo.

"Okay, just asking, not complaining. Lord, what a man."

"You said that once tonight."

"Sure, but I didn't know from nothing then."

She asked for the clothes hamper, got directions, and came back to the living room tastefully draped in a sort of Roman toga or something made of a clean sheet, and she looked good enough to eat. She slid down beside me and took a long, slow drink. "Boy, that's good. Most people do too much drinking too early and get too foamed up. That's against the best performance. The best time for a drink is right now."

Being in agreement, I nodded, not mentioning that I had been pretty well tanked most of the night. I pulled her to me and held her close. I had a terrific affection for this great big hunk of shapely gal. She could back up to her man and fight like a wildcat, then turn to him and love him to a flat frazzle. I wasn't frazzled yet, but I had a few loose seams. We came up for needed air, and turned our attentions to our drinks for a while.

"Prett, what the devil are you working at that joint for?"

"Why does any girl work?"

"That's stock, but it ain't any good. You have looks, you're sharp as a tack, you're fine gathering of a woman, you're good looking, and you've got personality. Why hasn't some guy copped you off?"

"The places I work, I guess. I went through the sixth grade and don't have a lot of ambition." She sighed. "I find a man like you—kind, considerate, probably too generous—you like my kind, and we make the best sort of hay together. That's all it ever amounts to. Answer your own question. Why wouldn't you cop me off?"

I lit a cigarette and inhaled deeply. "I'm thirty-three years old, Prett, and I fall in love regularly. I can't subject women to that sort of living. Suppose I'd fall in love with you...and that would be a dead cinch if I saw much of you."

"Then you'll do it, because I have every intention of seeing you as often as possible. The very sight of you makes me grow all crawly inside."

"All right. Suppose I fell in love with you, then in a month, meet some chick who'd give me the eye?"

"You would. You can't miss it."

"What'd you think, then?"

"Probably wouldn't like it. I've been married to a guy who was too good lookin'. Not like you, because you're just big and attractive, like a blooded horse. You're not pretty. This egg was, and anything with a chest, and a figure to back them up, could have him. I dumped him."

"There you have it. I haven't ever seen the girl I'd want to cleave to till death do us, and so forth."

She grinned. "Honey, you got yourself a partner. I'm not going to camp on your trail. You and me make music. Let's make it often, then if you find *her,* you won't hear a squawk from me."

I nodded. "It's a deal."

"I'm a realist. If I can't have all of you, then I'll take what I can get, when I can get it."

"What about a job?"

"I'll get one."

"Where?"

"Oh, there's a little squirt in Pasadena that's been after me about a job."

"And what else?"

She laughed. "He's a transparent little man. He fairly drools whenever he offers the job."

"And'll fire you when you refuse to play."

She took my cigarette and pulled on it. "I know this guy. I've known him for some time. I feel sorry for him, and I think sometimes I'm just what he needs. He has a wife with brown, crooked teeth, a vile temper, six children, and a mustache. I think I'd be heaven to him."

"What does he do?"

"He's a lawyer. He's got the lettuce."

"What could you do for him?"

"Plenty. I can file and type a little. With a little practice, I could get good. My old man was a lawyer, a poor one, and I used to type his stuff for him."

"And he died early and you had to find a job."

"That's right."

She was sitting stiffly, her shining, store-looking hair cascading over her shoulders and down by her cheeks, her head bowed with her clenched hands straight by her sides, a statue of sad womanhood. I looked at her for a moment, then I beckoned. "Come here."

She came, wonderingly, hesitantly, and I took her tenderly in my arms and kissed her with gentle affection.

She snatched her lips away, and leaned her head on my shoulder. "Are you trying to make a sissy out of me?" Then she cried hard, disengaged herself and, still sobbing spasmodically, looked up and smiled. "That's what I needed. I know I'm a good lay, but I haven't had anyone who was gentle with me in years."

"Can it," I said, shortly, "and get you a face wash."

She went back to the bathroom, throwing the sheet aside, and splashed about in the lavatory for a while, coming back with her face shiny and her eyes clear.

She sat beside me, leaning her face thoughtfully against my shoulder, showing me that she could dally a bit, too.

She reached up and kissed me hard. "Too soon?"

I didn't answer, but swept her off the couch and carried her to the bedroom, where we proceeded to ruin the fresh bed make.

It must have been two hours later when a car slowed and stopped somewhere in the block, but I was too dazed and comfortable to pay any attention to it, since there were houses all along the street on one side, and cars are no curiosity. This one turned out to be interesting to me, however, when the bedroom lights went on and sprayed all over us.

"Up, you."

I sat up groggily and, after some effort, I made my eyes focus on my friend at The Brown House, where I had eaten that night. He held a P-38 with ease and experience, but a thick bandage on his neck showed that Prett had not smoked in vain, if not lethally.

"I said up, and you, too, you loose snipe."

I stared and played it a lot thicker than I felt, but Prett came awake and sat up, looking very alert and on her toes.

"What do you want?" she asked.

"Outside, Barden. You and me's got a date with an accident."

"Looks like you already had one."

"You kill me. Get off that bed and come with me. This has to look good."

"Who's the scaredest, you or Denkyn?"

"Talk away, chum, but get going. You got it built to perfection. Those extra nails won't help any."

I walked ahead and Prett followed similar orders while Bramlett stood there, grinning. "Fun, dope?"

"Hell, yes. I told Denkyn that was a stupid move to hire you in the first place, that old man Wenken was beginning to smell me. He said you were too stupid not to take a bribe."

"I can smell you from here," said Prett. "I could smell you at the House, that's why I wasn't having any."

"Particular chippy, aren't you?"

"You said it, jerk."

"Have fun, you two. It won't be long now."

"So you did Wenken in, too?" I put in, hoping wildly that something would happen, and I could have some info if it did.

His eyes narrowed. "Who said I did?"

"I do."

"What does it matter what you say? You aren't going any place that'll matter. People seldom fall from planes, but every now and then ..." He shrugged. "You know, suicide pact, letter written by you that all is lost and only the grave beckons in friendship."

"The day I write any letter for you, bud, hell will accommodate the Ice Follies."

He smiled thinly. "It suits me. That was just an added touch. This twist has had a foot-toasting coming for a long time. I think with you watching, the enjoyment will be double."

Well, there I was, or where was I? He tossed a shorthand notebook at me and tossed a pen along with it. "You can keep the pen."

"Thanks."

"Frank, don't do it."

"I can't let him burn your feet, Prett. He has us there. I want to see him get us in that plane."

"Even that has been thought of, chum. Our plans are perfect."

I held my breath so long I was sure the blood would burst from my face, but the shadow behind him came closer and closer, and finally a hand reached out, tweaking the P-38 from his hands like he was a child.

"Dear me," sighed Salvato, tolerantly, "when will you learn not to associate with rabble?"

Bramlett had shrunk back against the wall when his weapon had disappeared into thin air, and I struck him shoulder to shoulder. I wanted to get my hands on him and release the hell tiger in my guts. I hauled him around, and tried to tear the side off his face with a hook that had everything I possessed, but he took the sting from it on a shoulder, and I barked my knuckles on his head. He dug one into my with a whistling uppercut to my chin. I went backward, with him on top of me, just the right distance to get both feet in his chest at the end of a body snap. It tossed him backward against the wall, giving me time to get to my feet.

He came in, feinted me into a lead, and clipped me twice; once in the ribs, and once high on my already-cut cheek.

"You'd think I hadn't taught you that boxing was for gentlemen," complained Sam, mildly, tossing the pistol carelessly in the air. "And being no gentleman, you're not too hot at it."

The thought cleared the air and, in the next instant, I had Bramlett rolling on the floor in agony from a beaut of a shoe toe at the base of his kneecap.

"Ah ... so! I wondered," murmured Sam, pursing his lips, his calm, brown eyes still calm and brown. Nothing ruffles that guy.

A scream from Prett snapped us to. He had reached the night table, and had taken up my bronze ashtray with a football player standing in the middle of it. It was a god-awful weapon, and he rushed me with it. I was poised to dive under him, when Sam stepped out of the door and lashed a whiplike left into Bramlett's jaw that was traveling like an antitank shell. It cracked loudly, and sent my boy nosediving across the room, where he tried to butt the baseboarding into splinters. I shuddered as I thought what it would have been like to have been on the taking end of that one.

"To paraphrase an ancient ancestor, Sir Robert, the Bruce," began Sam, examining his knuckles like he would a questionably ripe herring, "I think I have broken my good battle axe."

"Pig's eye," I snorted, trying to quell the snakes leaping about in my belly. "This calls for a drink, and unless your hand has deteriorated no end, it'll be all right. I recall you hammering hot shells out of a 90 millimeter A.A. gun when the extracting mechanism failed."

"Eighth Defense Batallion," he murmured, disparagingly. "Their equipment wasn't up to snuff."

"Oh, Sam, this is Prett … er, what's your last name, Prett?"

"Vallance. You have no idea how glad I am to know you, Sam."

He bowed with a gallantry that made a fool of gravity. It always makes me giddy to see him do it.

"I am not without imagination, Miss," he said. "It is understandable."

We went into the living room, where I made healthy drinks for us, especially healthy for Sam. I had seen him give up in disgust in Frisco Chinatown one night after blotting up twenty seven whiskey sours at the Jade Palace, and not getting enough of a buzz to make his face feel funny. He's been off Chinese food ever since, blaming it for the failure of the liquor.

"Tell me how this visit came about?" I asked.

"Well, I was in town. You recall Mr. De Forest? He seems to think I'm the only man in Texas who knows how Romano should be stored."

"And, of course, he's wrong."

"Of course. He limits it to Texas. Romano, you know, in spite of its robust nature, is a temperamental cheese, and must be stored with care. It dries out and becomes hard very easily. Anyhow, he calls me and asks, as he does once or twice a month, if I'll bring him two pounds of Romano."

"Cripes, all the way from Dickinson to Houston with two pounds."

"If you'll just shut up for a moment. I wouldn't deliver just two pounds of cheese to you, but he always wants twenty or thirty dollars worth of other spaghetti supper items. Tomato paste, oregano, garlic, meatballs... I season and make them up myself... things like that."

"So that's why you're in Houston. Why are you here?"

"I had a twitter."

"What's that?" asked Prett.

"A twitter," pursued Sam, didactically, "is a presentiment, a psychic manifestation that all is not well... nay, allow me to correct that sentence. It only seems to be a psychic manifestation. Actually it might be better described as extra-sensory perception and, coming closer still, subconscious perception. In short, it was something I felt. Maybe I just wanted to drop by and see Frank, and discovered the presentiment after I saw that I was needed."

"The truth at last," I said.

"Well, I drove the pickup to the curb and stopped some distance short of the house, because I saw two evil-visaged men standing by the car in front of your house as I made my first inspecting run. Once parked, it was simple to come down that path back of the bushes on the vacant side of the street, approach the vehicle from their blind side, and dispose of them."

I perked up. "There were more?"

"Two more, as I have patiently related. Shall we view the remains?"

"Not now. We'd better go wrap Mr. Bramlett up and deliver him to the authorities."

"So that's who he is. I didn't recognize him. Bring some fishing cord along. I learned a certain, wonderful way of securing thumbs from a Jap officer, with fishing cord, that is most effective."

We went in, armed with fishing cord, but all we found was an opened window and a cool breeze billowing the curtains out.

"It all comes," said Sam, while I stood speechless with rage and futility, "of trusting the knockout too much. I should have thought he was good for an hour, but you never can tell. That Bramlett is one tough hombre." At that moment, the car out front roared into life, sped away, and was soon out of earshot.

I fell out with the reds and tramped back to the living room, where I made drinks and sat, looking morosely at the wall.

"Now," said Sam, softly, "you are in what Gordon McLendon likes to characterize as the pickle vat. That guy will shoot you on sight. What do you have on him, except the lease business? The way I see it, that's only a bit of underhanded finagling."

"I think he killed Wenken, and if I had him, I'd prove it ... the germ, talking about toasting Prett's feet."

"Such pretty feet, too," said Sam, looking admiringly at them. She tucked them out of sight beneath her, self-consciously.

"If I ever get my hands on him," I growled, "there'll be a foot-roasting like he never heard of. If that's the way he likes to work, he shouldn't mind too much if I work it on him."

"There is sound logic in what you say," remarked Sam, "but I rather doubt that he'd take kindly to any such program. I could be wrong, of course."

"I like Sam," said Prett, perkily. "He's the strong, silent type."

"You can no more deny him strength than you could a Percheron," I said, "but silent ... Holy cats!"

"By the way," said Sam, changing the subject, "have you been to see Coniver yet?"

"Not yet. The idea gives me a twitter. Now tell me who, exactly, was the culprit in that tax business."

"That'll probably never be known. The way I have it pictured is this: Denkyn makes a deal with Coniver, whereby a huge hunk of taxes are blown back or never collected. For this mild favor, Coniver is slipped ten thousand in unmarked bills, maybe more than that, depending on how much of the tax was fixed."

"How do you know about Coniver and Denkyn?"

Sam looked mysterious and blank. "That," he said, sententiously, "would be tattling. I used to have a half-step-neighbor-in-law who worked for the revenue department. He did a little extra-curricular figuring and came up with the dope, but he didn't say anything."

"Why? Why didn't he dig himself into the deal and gather some fish?"

"I think he felt sorry for Coniver, who has been over the bumps, what with a wife who went nuts and roasted their youngest child alive in a gas oven, and a daughter who married a beast. Well, this guy felt sorry for Coniver who is, I understand, a pitiable object and, in addition to his pity, didn't want to get caught in any avalanche of righteousness such as is now being pumped into the department by main force and awkwardness. One thing. If you can, be gentle with the old man. I have an idea he has suffered enough for one lifetime and, who knows, maybe he needed the money."

"I don't persecute people needlessly. Say, do you think there is any connection between the Coniver gal and her brother, who works for Denkyn, and this man?"

"I think it's a coincidence. This Coniver did have some other children, and an adopted daughter, but I doubt that they'd be fooling around with Denkyn. I could be wrong, of course."

"Well, according to this chick, she's hovering around Denkyn so as to splay him on the deck. Couldn't he have put pressure on Coniver, and made him jump through hoops?"

"Possibly. He could have discovered other malfeasances, and might have blackmailed him to his own advantage. Well, I must amoseying be." Sam got up, shook hands with Prett, and turned to me with a pained expression on his face. "As pleased as I am to have been of some slight assistance tonight, leave us not make this a habit. A twitter might fail me in a pinch."

"Scram … but thanks a lot, too."

He bowed to us, and left the room like an old world courier.

"I like him," repeated Prett. "He's sharp as a tack and twice as dangerous, which he hides under his soft way."

"He's a one man wave of destruction," I said. "He pulled me out of so many scrapes in the war, that it got plumb monotonous."

Prett stretched and yawned. "You can take me home if you want to. It's three o'clock."

"Suppose I don't want to?"

Her grin was big, showing her strong white teeth to advantage. "If not, what are we sitting around in here for?"

"Now you're talking my language. Let's go."

It was eight-thirty next morning, when she woke me with a tray of chow that was fit for a king. There were country smoked sausages, a mound of golden, scrambled eggs, and a side platter of hashed browns that made my mouth water.

"Cradle this tray on your legs while I go get the coffee pot."

"Hey, what about you?"

"I eat coffee and toast for breakfast, and I've et."

She came back with a pot of nectar, and chattered for fifteen minutes about this and that while I stuffed myself.

"By the way, where is your home town?"

"Sugar Lake. Why?"

"Just wondered. I thought maybe you might be from some other part of the world. You don't talk like a Texan."

"Some don't."

"Look, I'm being bribed to do something I'm not going to do. Why don't you take that money?"

"Nope. I'll make it."

"I'm not doing anything I'm not able to do."

"I won't take it."

"Alright, but let's look at it this way: You've given me just about the most wonderful night of my life and you won't let me make it up to you. I'm not trying to pay you. Why not accept it as a favor from one friend to another?"

"What makes you think I've given you more than you gave me? I thought that, at least, was obvious."

"Oh hell, I guess it was, but I'd still like to do something for you."

"You stay healthy, all in one piece, and let's have other nights like this once in a while. That's all I want from you."

I looked her up and down for a moment. Every time she moved, she'd slip around in her dress in a manner that made me want to stop eating. I did after a while, took a shower and shaved, while she washed the dishes and tidied up the kitchen. I came back, camped out on the bed again, and waited. She came in after a while, took one look at me, and grinned. "You're a man after my own heart. Wait till I shower."

"I'm a man and I'm not after your heart," I shot back.

She came in after five minutes of splashing, and caught me in a grip like a vise. She was cool and damp, but the dampness was soon evaporated.

Two hours later, I put her down at the neat little apartment house in Pasadena, where she lived.

"Frank, thanks for a wonderful night. I don't mean any one thing, not the sex alone, which you might say was enough, but everything. Your trouble, being able to help a little, meeting Sam, hearing about what you're doing, being able to feel concerned about you... and probably most of all because of the way you treated me... like a lady."

"Why shouldn't I have? You are a lady. You're honest, on the level, and... jeepers."

Her smile was misty. "Thanks, and give me a ring. I'm in the book."

"I'll do that soon, Prett. I'll want to know how you come out on the job."

I pondered over the case of Prett all the way to Laporte. Gals like her were as scarce as trees in Pasadena.

CHAPTER EIGHT

I found Coniver's house without any trouble. It was a modest little place, neat, and kept like you'd expect a man of advanced years with time on his hands to keep a yard. I didn't have a lot of enthusiasm about this end of the business, but it had to be done if I wanted to wrap this thing up as it should be.

I walked up on the little porch and knocked. A teenager, dressed as teenagers will, came to the door and nodded politely, getting ready to close the door if I started a pitchman's routine.

"Hi, sis. Is your father home?"

"Yes, sir, but he's taking a nap right now. He takes naps just before lunch. Won't you come in?"

I grinned. "So you'll entertain me until he wakes?"

She smiled back at me. "I'll try."

"Then what say we sit in the swing? Voices might wake him."

"Okay. I'm Danessa Coniver."

"I'm Frank Barden. One of these days, we'll be glad we met."

She giggled as we walked toward the swing. She could have been Dene's sister. She was five-two or three, and plumped out like nobody's business. The way she wore jeans wasn't too different from most females just climbing forth into flower; she had the legs unevenly rolled, and the rough cloth fit skin-tight across her derrière; but her breasts, not yet having attained their seniority, were as sharp as ice cream cones and the plaid shirt, with the tail swinging free, couldn't nearly come in at the waist. It was supported too far out in front.

"You're thinking," I said, as we sat in the swing, "that this is a little out of your line, entertaining grown-ups, and you're wondering how it's done."

She flushed and giggled again. "Yes, sir, I was thinking something like that."

"Well, I'm not hard to entertain. Tell me about your football team."

She shrugged. "I don't care a lot about football. The players are so whreepy."

I goggled. "Whreepy?"

"Sure. You know, scroups."

"Ah, now all is clear. Are all of them like that?"

"No. Not all. Take Jesse Spracklin. He made all-state last year. He's an "A" student, and a gentleman. I like him. In fact, he has asked me to go to the Senior Prom with him, but I can't."

"Why?"

She looked away. "Well, it's sort of a family secret."

"Anything to do with a new evening dress?"

Her face paled, and I thought for a moment she'd dash back into the house. "The first time, I thought you were just … but twice … you're reading my mind." Her shoulders slumped. "My father doesn't have a lot of money, Mr. Barden. I can't ask him for a new evening dress."

"And you'd rather go than anything in the world right now, wouldn't you?"

Tears came to her eyes. "Yes, sir, but I'm young and I can stand it. I just can't go, and that's the end of it."

"Wanna bet?"

She looked at me, and I was grinning from ear to ear. "I don't understand."

"You say you can't go; I say you can. What if they'd call you up from Weilmann's, in Houston, and tell you that you had the pick of the place, and that they'd pay your bus fare, and that of a friend of yours if you'd come pick it out?"

She was silent for a while, peeling scarlet lacquer from a thumbnail, her adolescent breasts heaving distractingly. "Weilmann's … Houston … but—" She looked up at me, blinking the tears away. "But they wouldn't do something like that."

"Tell you what; if they don't, then I'll buy you an evening dress."

She still couldn't believe it, and shook her head. "Pop wouldn't let you buy me a dress."

"Who says I'm buying it?"

"Well, someone surely would."

"Not necessarily. Storekeepers have hearts like other people."

She punched a pink palm with a pink forefinger so hard that her dark hair danced silkily on her shoulders. "You know very well that no storekeeper is going to pick me, out of all the girls around Houston, to give a hundred dollar evening dress."

"Look. Suppose you just let it happen, and not ask too deeply into the details. Your father could not object to someone giving you an evening dress … especially if the notice came from the store that it was already bought and paid for … as well as your bus fare from here to Houston."

Her eyes grew wet again as she held them up to mine. "And to think," she whispered, "I almost slammed the door on your foot."

"Okay, it's settled?"

"Yes sir, and don't think I don't know." A sob wracked her slender frame, but that was all. "I'll go see if Pop's awake. He should be."

When Douglas Coniver came out on the porch, I almost bid him the time of day and left, but I was in too deeply then, so I got up, told him my name, and shook his hand.

He was slim and spare, with a scattering of colorless hair and a lined, weak face that showed his age.

"What can I do for you, Mr. Barden?"

"Mr. Coniver, I have a job to do that I don't like. It involves dragging up old follies, but I seem to have no alternative. What can you tell me about Thaddeus Denkyn?"

The old man swayed, and sat in the swing with a bounce. "It had to come out ... it had to come out, I suppose. Who are you, a government man?"

"No, sir. I'm an investigator who has been retained by Wenken, Denkyn, and Nodd for a purpose I haven't been as yet able to ascertain. I think there is some tremendous dodge in the making, and I rather expect to be a whipping boy. That's why I'm working at this matter; that, and because Mr. Wenken is dead ... murdered, and I think by someone in that organization."

"Wenken dead? Why, he was a fine man." Sweat dewed his pale brow. "He even warned me once ... I don't know how he knew, that I was playing with fire." Now that the ice was broken, and Coniver found that arrest was not imminent, he seemed to relax. "What can I tell you, Mr. Barden?"

Now that he asked, I wasn't too sure what to ask, so I shot something at him that had been nudging me for several days. "Mr. Coniver, what sort of hold had Denkyn on you?"

He went pale, and his hands trembled to the point of jerking as he tried to get a cigarette to his mouth. "W-w-why do you ask?"

"Is it true?"

Sweat started out of his forehead. "Please, I'd like to talk to you, but I can't. I'm old, and I don't matter any more, but my family ... he has them in the palm of his hand. My daughter is his secretary, and my son, his chauffeur. Mr. Barden, I know this must sound dramatic and foolish, but do you know that Thaddeus Denkyn could have either of them murdered, at any time, and he'd never even be arrested?"

"I can believe it. I have even seen myself in the role of executioner—unwillingly, but surely you don't have enough money that he can blackmail you on account of that tax business?"

"You think that? Let me tell you … no, I can't." His breath caught like a sob.

"Now, look here. My word to you is nothing; I admit that, because you don't know me. However, I'll tell you anyway. Denkyn's star is going down, and I'm the night that'll cover it." I was being dramatic myself, but it was needed. I could see that.

"He, or some of his people, have stooped to murder," I continued, "and whether I get him or not, someone will. I know your daughter, and I've met the younger one. I'm in sympathy with you, because I know something of your history. If you help me in this, I'll help you. If you don't, you stand a chance of getting into it anyway. With me at the wheel, you can be kept out of it. If the law has to do it their way, they'll tear down everything, look over the pieces, and start building again. That's where you'll come in."

He looked like a shriveled bag of bones huddled in the swing. Tired, old, and defeated. "What can I tell you?" he asked, hoarsely.

"You were paid a sum while with the Department, to juggle the tax records of Thad Denkyn, weren't you?"

"Yes. In ten years time, I saved him half a million dollars. Out of that, I received twenty percent. Since then, under threat of exposure, he has taken back most of it. I have a small income which he doesn't know about, or I believe he'd take that, too."

"Would not exposing you, also expose him?"

"Not the way we did it. I was a fool not to protect myself. I won't bore you with the details, but exposing it would reflect on the department and me; not on him."

"What about the others, Nodd and Wenken?"

"Of Nodd I know nothing, except that he's a pretty slick article. He's been on the carpet several times. Wenken always paid to the last cent. Of course, he had the ranch, and that helps a lot. We never even had to write him a letter. He was punctual and completely honest. Any number of times we refunded sizable amounts because he wouldn't risk borderline deductions." His eyes brightened, pitifully. "The worst thing yet is now in the making. I have a nephew working for the department in a job similar to mine. Denkyn is trying to make me persuade the boy to do for him as I did. He threatens all sorts of things."

"Don't worry, Mr. Coniver. Denkyn won't last long. He's had luck, but it's run out."

"I wish I could believe that. I wish I could."

"There is one thing you must believe. I'll do everything in my power to see that you don't come in for any more knocks. I'm on your side. That's what I want you to believe."

He sighed. "Very well. You have given me something almost like hope."

"I'm glad of that. Tell me, does Denkyn ever come to see you?"

"No, we meet at his lodge on Lake *Poule D'eau*."

"Will you call me the next time he wants to have a meeting?"

"There's supposed to be one tomorrow night, and the thought of it makes me sick. I fully expect to be found floating in that lake some day. I will *not* involve my nephew in any such sordid business as I was once a party to."

"You can forget that. I'll be at that lodge tomorrow night."

"You will?"

"I will…and there's another thing. I'm going to buy your daughter an evening gown for her Prom."

"Oh, no. I couldn't allow that."

I got up and pulled him to his feet by the shirt, smoking him with a stare. "Is that so? Well, isn't that something? Pride that will allow a man to defraud the government of half a million dollars in revenue, accept a hundred-thousand-dollar bribe, and live in fear of exposure, is too tender to accept a mere bagatelle like an evening dress, which you were stupid enough not to buy yourself. Okay, Coniver. I'll just let you face Denkyn tomorrow night by yourself. People turn blue when they've been in the water a long time, and the crabs and fish eat the eyes and ears off while time tenderizes you enough so they can get at the rest."

He clapped his hands to his face and sank back into the swing, his thin shoulders shaking with revulsion and terror.

"Do I give the kid an evening dress?"

"Yes ... yes ... do anything you wish, but don't make me face Denkyn alone. I don't think I could stand it, now that you've given me hope."

"It's a deal, and not a word to Danessa."

"No, I won't say a word ... not a word."

"When the letter comes from the dress shop, you'll be pleased and surprised. Get it?"

"Yes, yes, of course ... anything."

"Okay, I'm on my way. You won't see me or hear from me unless I'm needed. Understand?"

"Yes ... yes."

"I'd advise that you gas yourself up a bit, and stand him down. Rub it in. Sneer at him, curse him for every sort of low dog you can think of ... you must have wanted to do that for a long time."

Coniver seemed to stiffen, and his eyes glittered. "You'll be backing me up?"

"All the way. You can depend on it."

He stood up and gripped me like a man who has seen the light after solitary confinement.

"Thank you, son. You've given me confidence. I feel better than I have for months."

I grinned and tapped him briskly on one thin shoulder. "That's the way, Doug."

He flushed a little. "No one's called me that, except my wife, for years."

"You're Doug, from now on. Now go in, take a stiff jolt of brandy to whet your appetite, and eat a good meal. Then take another nap. Everything's in the bag."

I watched him go through the door that never got a chance to slam. Danessa ran out, took a quick look through the parlor, then dashed into my arms and, tiptoeing, planted a very unadolescent kiss on my lips. She had intended it, as I guessed, to be a quickie, but somehow it didn't work out that way, and it shook us both to the roots of our hair. She drew away an inch or so, her eyes opaque with shock and question, then she buried her soft young mouth in mine again and I had to break us.

"Hey, suppose Jesse should see us?"

She smiled tremulously, her uneducated lips quivering, and deep dimples showing in her cheeks. "Who cares? I just wanted to thank you for being so swell, but it sort … sort of …"

"Got away from us?"

"That's right. Now I wish *you* were taking me."

"Tell you what. When you come to Houston, give me a buzz and I'll take you and your friend to the Shamrock for cocktails, dinner, and dancing."

She gave a little shriek. "You will?" She leaped in the air and turned completely around.

"Oooooo, but that'll be super!" She grew serious. "But suppose I really love you, like I feel like I do right now?"

I laughed and stroked her soft hair. "So what? All you have to do is grow two years in one, and all I've got to do is stand still, and you'll catch up with me in no time; then we can get married."

Her laughter rang out happily. She was being kidded and knew it, but it didn't cast any gloom. "I still think you're wonderful; and I don't care what you say, I love you." Her face flamed, she turned, and fairly dove back into the house.

I drove back to Houston in a happy daze, the sort of golden glow a man feels when he's made someone else happy. I laughed at the thought, growled at it, then cussed Denkyn out loud. "Best use your stinkin' money ever went for," I said, to the road ahead, "even if it is bribe money." When I got home, there he was, pacing up and down, wearing out my front yard, whacking himself on the thighs with a pair of yellow pigskin gloves.

"Where've you been?" he demanded, angrily, as I stepped from the car.

"Smooth out, Croesus, or I'll have to slap some respect into you," I said, like a toughie. I had my bluff on him, and I wasn't letting go of it now.

"Don't forget, you're working for me," he said, viciously.

"Yeah, you'd like to forget it, wouldn't you?"

"What do you mean?"

"I get asked that all the time. I think I was fairly clear."

He bit his thick underlip, and blinked at me for a moment. "I thought I told you to lay off Bramlett?"

"So you did, and so I did; but if he's your boy, you'd better tell him to lay off me or I'll make a pretzel out of him." I pointed to the patch over my left eye, and the knot on my head.

"Now I want to tell you something about your precious Bramlett. He answers the description of the man who shot Wenken. I'm to bring him in, remember?"

"Yes," he nodded, thoughtfully. "Yes, of course."

"Unless," I suggested, nastily, "you want to go on record as calling me off that, too."

"I don't like the tone of your voice, Barden."

"And I don't like the way your face is screwed on."

He breathed deeply. "I'm not accustomed to employees talking like that to me."

"That's because they depend on you for a living. If it wasn't you, there'd be others ... for me."

"Yes. Well, we shouldn't quarrel."

"Right. You'll never know when you'll need me to set up an income tax deal for you ... with all my Washington connections."

His face slowly went putty-colored, showing up purple veins in his nose. "I don't like jokes like that, Barden. I wouldn't play it too loose with me, if I were you."

"Neither would I, if I were you, Jackson. I think I'd better tell you more about Bramlett. He came here last night to put me in the daisies. I don't know how much you knew about the project, but the next time I get my hands on him, I'm going to stake him out in the marsh and build a fire on his belly. I'll find out things he never even knew."

"That's not lawful," said Denkyn, getting some of his color back, "and I'd advise against it."

"It's against the law to sap citizens from the back, then try to take them for airplane rides where the passenger is supposed to fall out."

"He was joking."

"The joke was entirely lost on me. Luckily, a friend of mine, whose back twitters in times of danger, came by and, together, we made some lovely hash of the prankster. Now let me tell you something for your own good. I can't prove you saw him, nor can I prove you know where he is, but I can promise you hot water— more than enough for an arthritis treatment if you know where he is and don't tell me."

"I don't know where he is."

"You didn't have to say that, but I expected it."

"Barden, are you trying to make a criminal out of me?"

I laughed in his face. "Why don't you can your sorry jokes and go home?"

He didn't go in a very good humor, but he went. I wished I had the power Danessa Coniver thought I had. I'd have read his mind, then and there, and shortened the case a lot, or so I figured.

I went in the house, made a fast turn, and came out mad as a hornet, because I had intended to go to Lake Poule D'eau and look the place over, but had driven by the Lake road deep in cogitation, and forgot it.

I was about to get in my car, when a Buick Riviera drove up, and an individual began to reel himself out until a full six-feet-six had emerged. He was topped by a cream white Stetson, a worsted shirt the same color, and doeskin trousers that hollered money as far as you could see him. His Justins caught the sunlight, and sparked like lacquer. All in all, I did a flash assay on his getup, and came up with about two hundred and ten bucks worth of clothes. That didn't include a .45 revolver the size of a small field piece with pearl handles. Ranger. I could have spotted him a long way off without the buzzer on his pocket. He was slicked out, as they are when they have private incomes, but here's a tip: Don't ever tangle with one.

This long gent flowed up my sidewalk and broke out a grin. "Roll out the carpet, boy, the great has arrived." He took off his hat, revealing a head of the kinkiest, red hair that ever flamed from a pate. I let out a roar, and we both met like a couple of tanks and began pounding dust, chips, and moths out of each other.

"Boy, come on in here and let me feed you some maiden milk." We went in, still acting like a couple of fools. It was "Roller" Lester who had played fullback, while I blocked for him. I hadn't seen him in ten years, and it took me a while to tumble. When he took off that hat, though, I dug him good.

We blatted like a couple of hebephrenic sheep for half an hour, then it occurred to me that he might want something.

"Is this social, or business? You never looked me up before."

"Call it social business. I'm head of the district, but when I heard who was mixed up in Wenken's passing, I beat it out here myself."

"Why you, and not the county law?"

"Well, the county law isn't too hot, and admits it. They never have anything happen out there—maybe a Mex snaffling a sheep and such and, as Wenken used to say: 'Anybody who'd own a sheep, deserves to have 'em stolen.' Wenken was one of the hottest operators we ever had in his younger days, and could thumb out six shots from a Frontier model faster than a tommy gun. Our interest is sort of personal. What do you have on it?"

"Pick up a bird name of Harold Bramlett, who used to buy leases for Wenken's company. He's the one who answers the description of the murderer. Here of late, I've thought maybe there was a chance that he didn't do it, but a good sweat session might bring all sorts of things to the surface. Such as why he wanted to do away with me last night."

"Uh oh, as bad as that, hunh?"

"That's bad enough. I was saved by a whisker. I pulled a fool stunt and let him know I suspected him of piloting the plane that is involved. He tried to sap me not long afterward, and that night he came in here, he held me up and was about to make it good, when a friend of mine stopped in."

He opened a notebook, made a few notations, then snapped it to. "Got anything to add to that?"

I took a deep breath, pondered a moment, then nodded. It might be a good idea to have him on my side, so I told the whole works, without using Coniver's name … which he questioned me about.

"Nup. I've told you the whole works, so be satisfied. I've promised the old man I'd keep him out of it. He's suffered plenty, and he has a couple of fine kids who don't deserve to be kicked around just because their old man is a fool. That part of it's ancient history, anyhow."

He sighed briefly. "That's the way you private birds like to operate. We can't."

"Don't kid me, son. How many times have you been ordered to lay off?"

He paled a little, and his steel blue eyes got hard as diamonds. "It happens," he said, softly, like a tiger whispering. "So far it hasn't come down to me, personally. When it does, you'll hear the explosion further than they did Bikini."

I believed him. You didn't push guys like Lester around, either physically, or any other way. "By the way," I said, feeling a rising excitement, "could you let me have a very small, sensitive, compact wire recorder for tomorrow?"

He looked at me closely. "You going to put it up at Denkyn's lodge?"

"That's right. I might catch some good music."

He grinned, showing crooked, but very white teeth. "Son, I like the way you operate. Why don't you go to work for us?"

I shook my head. "I'm solo now. My own boss. I worked for Uncle a while, until I got to where I couldn't bear the sight of my boss. I don't take orders well."

"So I remember from the dear, dear football days. Well, good luck." He wrote a few words on a slip of note paper, and tore it from the book. "Go to Sub Station G—you know where it is—and tell Ed Snow I said to let you have what you want. This note will fix it."

CHAPTER NINE

Lake Poule D'eau has one narrow connection with the Houston Ship Canal, and once in a while it is subjected to tides, so most of the lodges and camps are built pretty high from the ground.

I called Coniver before I left home, and he gave me directions. I now sat in my car facing the widest section of the lake, with Denkyn's lodge only two hundred yards farther down the narrow, graveled road. I got out and sat on the fender of the car with an unloaded camera in my hands, and went through the motions of making pictures of the sunset that flamed like an overpainted trollop in the west. There was no activity around the nearer camps, but I didn't trust anything but the dark.

It seemed a long time coming, but patience was rewarded and an hour or so later, I was under Denkyn's stilted lodge, poking around the area near the fireplace, trying to find a knot or crack that would serve my purpose. The recorder was a small thing, the idea being to screw it to the wall, floor, or behind a door, as long as there was a way for the sound to get through the obstacle. Snow had showed me how it worked, and the sensitive mike was so good that a hole the size of a pencil was sufficient. You found the hole or crack, then screwed the instrument up to it. At a given time, you set it for recording, after which it would run for hours ... slow. It was operated by two, six-volt dry cells, and the wire spool was good for about eight hours of reproduction. Nifty.

I had a pencil flashlight, which I was careful to hold as close to the flooring as I could to keep down reflection if anyone passed. After crawling around until I was hot, sweaty, and bushed, I still hadn't found anything, and was thinking about doing some house breaking, when a thought occurred to me as I poked my hand into a bed of soft ashes. The fireplace! It was too hot for fires and, in some manner, last winter's ashes had sifted down under the house.

I soon found out why. It was one of those modern fireplaces, with a sort of grate as a floor, so that all you had to do to move ashes was to slide the grate to one side, and the ashes would fall through. I raked the stuff aside until I could shine the light all the way through and see the blackened bricks of the chimney above. Perfect!

I felt around until I located a few loose bricks, and made a bed for the machine, out of sight, but with plenty of open area for good recording. I didn't set it, because I'd be with it the next night, I was sure.

My bathroom looked like hell after I finally got the grime off me, and I was about as hungry as a man ordinarily gets without cramping. I called a sea food place called Lippman's, and told them to broil me the biggest flounder they could find … slowly, with butter, along with a couple of Idaho spuds, baked till the jackets were crisp, and to get along with it because I'd be there in fifteen minutes and, if it wasn't ready, I'd eat the nearest waitress.

I was dressed in a cool, cream-colored nylon cord, with a tall, diluted *Donna Angel* in my hand, when the phone rang. I was afraid to answer it because I certainly wasn't going to put off my dinner any longer and it might spell trouble, but I did, anyway.

"Hello."

"Mr. Barden?" Oh boy, what a voice. You could have churned it and gotten butter.

"Er … yes … Say, isn't that Marlo?"

"Yes. Mr. Barden, could I talk to you?"

"Why, of course, but I've been banned from the ranch, remember?"

It sounded like a muffled sob at the other end, which made me ache deep in the throat. "Please, don't make fun of me. I'm very sorry about that."

"Sure, kid. Where are you?" I felt like crying myself.

"I'm at the Rice."

"Well, I'm starving, and I'm about to eat."

"Where?"

"At Lippman's. It's way out Milam..."

"Yes, I know where it is. It'll save time if I catch a taxi and meet you there, if you don't mind."

"Not in the least. I'll be delighted. Shall I order for you?"

She hesitated. "I don't think I could eat much."

"Nuts. I'll work one of my famous gustatory miracles. You'll eat. When have you eaten last?"

"I...I don't know, really. I drank a glass of milk..." Her voice trailed off.

"I'll be there when you get there."

I was, with a quart of *Donna Angel* in my pocket, which I handed over to René Voisin, the amiable proprietor, who promised to treat it with the proper reverence according to directions.

I wasn't prepared for the Marlo who came in Lippman's that night. She dressed very simply in something soft and blue and clinging, strapless, with a little white piqué jacket that was not intended to button (which was a good thing, it'd never have made it) with short sleeves and a sort of miniature sailor collar. The neckline dipped a lot lower into the cut between her breasts than I would ever have thought she'd tolerate, and the effect was to turn the miss-meal cramp in my stomach into a cramp of vastly different sources and intensity.

I stood up and took her hand, noticing that she had been crying. "Something wrong, kid?"

The string snapped for a moment; she cried hard against me, then abruptly stiffened and smiled tremulously. "Damn sissy! I'm sorry."

"I'm not. You've needed to do that for some time."

She sat across from me, regarding me through damp eyes that looked like crushed violets and as deep as Spindletop Gusher, with an entire, magnificent woman reflected in their depths. I prickled all over as though I had seen grandma in her drawers, or watched an evil man wrestle with his soul.

"Yes, I've needed that. I allowed other considerations to build a fence between us. I shouldn't have done that."

"It is understandable. You were unfortunate in catching me unawares... or I was unfortunate."

"I'm afraid I wasn't conditioned for it. I didn't expect it."

"Why? Did I impress you as a choir boy?"

"On the contrary, I was certain you weren't."

"But still you were shocked and maybe disappointed?"

"I guess so." She gestured distastefully. "I don't know." Her breath caught in her throat.

"Look, Marlo, where's Wilbur?"

She turned perplexed eyes on me. "Who?"

"Wilbur, John, Percival. Surely there's a guy you care a lot about, who should be rallying around at a time like this."

She looked at me so long I felt like lighting a shuck and high-tailing it. Then she shook her hand slowly. "No, there's no one. I don't think you believed me when I told you about Harold."

"I guess I did, but you just don't seem the type. We won't go into it now, anyhow. Was there something special you wanted to talk about?"

Her eyes dropped, and she drew lines in the table cloth with her fork, her chin trembling a little. I gulped and made a furious motion to Voisin. He trotted to the table.

"Are the private rooms filled?"

"For you, Frank, they is wide opens. Come this way."

I took her by the arm and led her across the floor into a cozy, private dining room with a small couch and a small, round table in the center of which rested a candle as big as a baseball bat with a pot-bellied lamp chimney over it. Voisin lit it, seated us, then turned out the overhead lamp. It was very quiet in there, until at last we could hear the strains of soft, Spanish music filtering in through a speaker that I couldn't locate. Voisin is an incurable romantic.

"Now, kid, what's on your mind?"

She held her head up, beautiful past all reality in the ruddy glow of the candle, her hair glinting softly. "This is hard to say, because I've been rude to you, but Frank, I don't have anyone any more. I have some friends, and the men at the ranch have been kind, but ..." She shook her head distractedly. "It's terrible not to have *anyone,* and I just couldn't stand it at the ranch any more ... alone."

"I know," I said, softly. "And you came straight to me."

She nodded, biting her lips to quell their trembling. "But why? I hardly know you. I don't even know why I do things any more."

"It makes me feel good that you did. I'm glad. If I were less a scientist, I'd call it woman's intuition."

"The intuition wasn't shocked," she said, a little breathlessly, "at that scene in your home. Just the conventional, conscious me." She bent her head over and wept bitterly for some time, then she dried her eyes, and blew her nose softly. "I won't do that again."

"Got it all out that time?"

"I think so."

I punched the bell three times, and Voisin came in bearing two tall drinks containing rum and certain other mysteries.

"Sip along on that," I told her, giving birth to a grin I hoped was wholehearted enough to give her a lift. She managed a smile in return, and took a long pull at her drink.

Mine lit an immediate fire in my empty stomach and, due to rapid absorption, had me tingling from head to foot in no time. She reacted similarly and, by the time the drink was consumed, her eyes were sparkling and her smile was an improvement over previous efforts.

She drained her glass and, reaching across the table, put a hand over mine. "Thanks, Frank," she said, huskily, "for being a good egg. You've been very considerate."

"And," I said, gallantly, "the fact that you're probably the most beautiful creature on earth hasn't a thing to do with it."

"I know it hasn't. That's what makes it wonderful."

"Don't believe it. If you'd had buck teeth and sour breath, I'd never have looked at you twice."

She was pure woman, and preened a little at that. "Do you think I'm beautiful?"

"Passably."

"Seriously, Frank."

"Seriously."

She took off her piqué jacket, exposing round arms, conditioned marvelously, with a muscle rippling softly here and there. Her back had that flawless surface that makes you wonder if it isn't made up; but all the make-up Marlo had on was a deft touch of lipstick.

"You know," she said, as she sat down again, "I think I could eat something."

I started. I had forgotten that I was hungry; I was starving. I rang the code for Voisin, and he responded so fast it seemed slightly magical.

When he came back, he brought steaming platters of broiled flounder with a big, green salad and side dishes of baked potatoes, gutted on top, and running with rich butter.

There wasn't any more talking for some time because those succulent flounders had too much on the ball. Marlo ate like a ranch hand, and in half an hour we were both practically foundered.

Voisin cleared away the dishes and brought us tiny glasses of Metaxa, which we sipped between sips of strong, pungent French-drip coffee.

"This is not only my first real meal in days, but an occasion I won't forget in a hurry. Frank, I couldn't have been sore at you because it's all gone now."

"That's the way. Men are men, you know."

"Do they have to be?"

"Spoken like a woman. Take the masculine drive away from a man, and what do you have? A capon. You wouldn't like that."

"No, I guess not."

"Right. I don't say that the hairy-chested male is without discommoding potentialities, but I do say if you take his hairy chest away from him, you don't have much left."

"What has hair to do with it?"

"Nothing. I was using it as a general term to indicate man as a creature that women attract, and plenty."

"You don't think it's wrong?"

"Morals were concocted by man. I was made like me. Either my maker was wrong in making me this way, or man is all wet in his conception of what the maker had in mind."

"You make it sound simple; so simple I can't see why the same thing shouldn't apply to women, too."

I grinned. "Some of them do feel that way. They're coming to see the light."

"I'm afraid you'll find me pretty confused about such things. I'm not very well up on the subject."

"Didn't you study about it in college?"

"Some, but you know how that is. Those things are always about the other fellow. It never really reached me."

"In my case," I said, not quite knowing where this was leading, "I've found my impulses pretty good pilots."

"Don't you ever think of the girl?"

"Invariably. That's an impulse, too."

"I see." She flushed suddenly, and fell silent.

"Come on, now," I urged, "don't clam up now. I'm your dutch uncle."

She held her head up. "I was just thinking of the times I've felt like following nature to the limit."

"I rather thought you had, at some time. Anyone as fitted for love as you could have hardly escaped some twinges, if only when you dry off after a bath in front of your mirror."

Her flush deepened, and she toyed with her brandy glass for a while. "I never felt it with anyone but Harold."

"And immediately afterward, you thought you were in love with him."

She gasped faintly, and looked at me a little fearfully. "How did you know that?"

"It's not unusual. Especially with inexperienced girls. And, after all, what is love, anyhow?"

She thought that over. "I've asked myself that before. I never came to the answer."

"What answer did you come to?"

Her shoulders lifted slightly. "Silly, romantic answers, I'm afraid."

There was more silence that, for some reason, did not seem uncomfortable. We were just thinking, and words weren't necessary.

"Frank, what's happening, I mean about my father's murderer? A tall redhead talked to me yesterday, and I got the impression that the Rangers are interested."

"They are," I said, and brought her up to date. When I had told her all, I inserted the knife. "But for a major miracle, I'd be dead now. If that doesn't show you Mr. Bramlett in all his unlovely details, I don't suppose there's any use trying any more. I am beginning to doubt that he is the murderer, but the thought doesn't revolt him. The order is out to pick him up for questioning."

She slumped dejectedly. "I've been thinking about him lately. I see many things I hadn't been able to see before."

"May I ask an impertinent question that's none of my business?"

"Certainly."

"How serious was your affair with him?"

She tried to entice another drop of fluid from the glass, then put it down. I rang for Voisin, who appeared in a flash, like a gnome, bearing duplicates of the drinks we had had before dinner.

When the door closed, her eyes raised to mine. "He tried ... all the way. He almost succeeded, several times, but not quite ... I wonder ..."

"What?"

"Oh, sometimes I think I was foolish."

"Honey, you were foolish when you let him get you the way he did."

"No, I mean ... Frank, there's not too much happiness in life. Why should we resist any of it?"

I pondered for a moment. "In the case of Bramlett vs Wenken, I'd say that your resistance prevented a much more serious reaction that would have come later. As it is, you'll suffer some pain, but nothing to what you would have if it had gone to the limit. I know."

"I guess you're right. Lately, I have re-lived those occasions in my mind and asked myself why I didn't give in. There doesn't seem to be an answer."

"There's an answer, maybe several. Your environment, for one thing, and that instinct you seem to have. When you met me, you received an impression, maybe a subconscious one. I make bold to say it was a good one. Later, events changed it. Later still, you were forced to embrace the original opinion. In spite of the excellent spot in your affections held by Bramlett, in spite of the wholly natural desire to give in, there was some little discord deep in your subconscious that kept you from letting go."

"Frank, you make such wonderful sense." She was wide-eyed with admiration, and I did a slow pink job that made her laugh, rich laughter that rang heartily off the walls. "Why, you big, self-conscious sissy."

"Awww, hell, I got strung out there and hypnotized by the sound of my own voice."

"Just the same, I think it was marvelous. I feel free and light again." She drained her drink and thumped the glass on the table. "Fill 'er up, son. I haven't howled in a long time."

I summoned Voisin, who came through the door apologetically. "I'm all sorry to pieces, Frank, but the good rum she's been drunk up. I'm putting in some of mine, not so hot."

"M'seur Voisin. C'est tres bon," said Marlo, in surprisingly good French, making Voisin goggle, then grin.

"Je vous donne un cigarette," she continued, smiling, holding out a package.

He accepted one mechanically, and burst into a flood of Cajun too fast for me to catch, and they both fell out laughing when he finished. They lit each other's cigarettes, cross-armed, then laughed again. Everyone loved everyone else and all was swell.

Whatever might be said of the quality of his rum, Voisin had not stinted and, by the time we had finished, neither of us were feeling any pain. Marlo's face was flushed, and her eyes sparkling like gems. She tossed her short hair restively, then leaned back in her chair to stretch like a tigress. The effort almost turned her dress traitor, and I felt that my head was being squeezed between Salvato's powerful hands. She relaxed and they came back into place, leaving me feeling a little empty and disappointed.

I don't think either of us knew where we were going when we left Lippman's, but we were holding each other by the arm and laughing uproariously at something ... I don't know what, or maybe we'd have noticed that we were being observed.

We didn't, and sailed out on the street and scudded out Milam, going away from town. I don't know what caused me to suddenly notice the car, but I did, and I almost fainted because it was Bramlett on the side next to us, away from the driver, and he was pointing one of those short, double-barreled shotgun pistols at us that are sometimes carried by bank messengers. It is a lethal thing at short range when loaded with slugs or buckshot.

I yelled and went for my brakes, but that wasn't why he missed us. A black Buick kissed him from behind just as the gun went off and, instead of chewing me to bits, the charge spattered my windshield into fragments. I braked down as fast as I could without taking the ditch, but the other car wasn't so lucky. The collision had thrown it into a skid, and it went into the ditch, tried to climb out like a wounded animal, then started turning over. It smashed top-on into a telephone pole, cracked it, and leaned it to one side like a broken leg.

The Buick stopped even with us and Roller Lester slowly poured out on the highway, his hat askew, but his face split with a grin.

"Babes in the wood," he said, pulling out a .45 with pearl grips that glinted beautifully in the moonlight.

Marlo and me hopped out, and the three of us approached the wrecked Chrysler. The driver we could see, all except his head, which was pinioned against the ground out of sight, and we could imagine what it looked like. Bramlett was draped uncomfortably over the back seat, his hand still clutching the short gun.

"Just as you thought," said Roller, as he hoisted him out of the car and dropped him on the grass. "He was sure layin' for you."

"Where did you come from?" I asked.

"We've been laying for him, too. I've had a man on you ever since I left your house. You were followed about ten blocks by this Chrysler, so my man put in a call for me when the car stopped here. That cinched the suspicion that he was following you. Still, I wanted to make sure, so I waited until you left and, when he took out after you, I knew. You went so fast I thought you'd lose me."

"Get yourself a good automobile," I jibed.

"I've got one. You just took off like a ruptured duck and, after all, I was driving without lights." He examined Bramlett and found nothing but a bumped head. We chatted until he came to, when he sat up, holding his head.

Marlo, who had been standing by silently until now, came closer and looked at the man hard.

"You missed me, Harold," she said, harshly.

He looked up groggily. "I wasn't trying to get you."

"Tell that to the fairies, you murderer."

"You think I killed your old man?"

"Who else? I understand the Rangers have ways to find out, though, especially when someone murders an old Ranger. I commend you to their tender care."

It seemed that Bramlett paled even whiter when he heard that.

"Let's bring it closer home," said Roller, in a hard voice. "Why were you shooting at Barden?"

"Try to find out, copper."

"We will," said Roller. "We will." Neither of us was prepared for his sudden break, but at least one of us was equal to it, so he managed to get about two steps gone before Roller reached out, and the long .45 barrel smacked him across the temple. He slid into a heap in the ditch just as the next car came up.

"Y'all lost us," panted the man, as he ran over. "We took the wrong turn."

"Put the cuffs on him and pack him in," said Roller. "Better get something on that cheek, Miss B." None of us had noticed it, but her cheek was bleeding, and had ruined the jacket and dress. It wasn't very deep, but bleeding freely. I took out my breast pocket handkerchief and made her hold it to the spot.

"We'll get along, Roller. You won't need me tonight, will you?"

"No. Like to have you down the first thing in the morning, though."

"Right. I'll be there."

"Now to get you to my house and a clean up job. If you went in the Rice like that, they'd call the cops."

"The dress was sort of old," she said. "It doesn't matter. I wonder if there's any glass left in it?"

"We'll see."

There wasn't; just a clean, shallow scrape that had bled more than a wound that size should. By the time we got home, it had stopped bleeding, but I examined it carefully, put Phemerol on it, and covered it with a bandaid.

"Now Dr. Barden prescribes a tonic, which he shall fix at once."

It helped to dispel the horrors that had effectively sobered us, but we were pretty quiet for a while.

"You are in the presence of a pretty big fool, Frank. Even after you told me what Harold did last night, it didn't make the sort of impression it should."

"And now?"

"Even I am not that big a fool."

"Let's don't hear you suggest that any more, honey." I got up from the chair and sat beside her on the couch. I put a hand over her strong, brown fingers. "I mean that. No more saying what a big fool you've been. Everyone is at some time."

She twisted on the couch as though in pain, and a frown creased her forehead. "Frank, *tell* me, why are you so sweet to me? I've been rude and haughty to you. I have no claim to your time or your interest."

I lifted my hands and let them drop. I hadn't thought too much about it, but it did seem I was turning into a regular Santa Claus. Three women, lately, had roughed the callous veneer off me and discovered a depth of reaction to human frailty, suffering, and bad luck that was astounding. Danessa, Prett, and Marlo.

"I don't know," I said, in a low voice. "I seem to have been born with a latent streak of softness." Then I said something that I can't account for. I sometimes suspected Salvato of being in the wings of the stage, using me as a dummy. It didn't even sound like me. "Maybe it's because I love you."

She started like a filly gigged in the flanks with a spur. "Frank, you don't mean that. Please don't play with me."

I didn't say anything, just sat there dumbfounded at my statement. I felt cold chills tear strips of hide off my back; tendons tightened like hawsers, and the palms of my hands were wet and uncomfortable.

"Play? Me?" I was Salvato's dummy again, but I didn't seem to have enough will to stop it. If this kept up—. By a supreme effort, I sat straight and looked at her, objectively.

She was curled up, as women will when seated on anything big enough, her eyes wide and filled with a mixture of astonishment and disbelief.

"What's wrong with it?" I asked, with unnecessary harshness. I had to be harsh or my voice would have squeaked up and down the scale like a late-turning adolescent's.

"Wrong? I don't know that anything's wrong with it. It's just that..." Then she threw it at me, and I fielded it like a hot brick. *"Do* you love me, Frank?"

I sat there and made a few passes at a breathless gulp. "Well, where a beautiful girl is involved..." Her eyes narrowed, and she got slowly to her feet.

"A beautiful girl. Is that all it takes? Just any beautiful girl?"

"Wait, now. I didn't say that."

"You haven't said anything, Frank," and before I knew it, the door had slammed behind her. I was so flummoxed that it must have been fifteen minutes before I realized that she was afoot, and almost busted a shin falling out of the house and getting into my car. No soap. I canvassed all the commercial places still open; drugstores, filling stations, and cafés, but no soap and no Marlo. Finally, I saw a taxi stand, drove in, and described her. The dispatcher hadn't seen anyone like that, but he was cooperative. He got on his short wave and, in three minutes, picked up a cab who was just about to discharge a customer at the Rice Hotel.

I gave him a ten spot for his trouble and crawled back to the house, undressed down to the skin in the living room, and sprawled on the couch with a tall, cold one.

CHAPTER TEN

When Prett came through the bedroom door and sat beside me, placing a cool hand on my thigh, it seemed the most natural thing in the world. It was an hour and some activity later before I asked: "How did you get in?"

She kissed me and wriggled closer, her hair smelling fresh and stimulating like newly cut clover. "I walked in. You have a bad habit of leaving your doors unlocked."

"You were here when we came in?"

"Yes. I heard it all. She's been hurt twice, Frank. I think you're a dope."

"Why?"

"You do love her, don't you?"

"I don't know."

"That's the way to get snafu if I ever heard it. You're all bound up in that personal outlook you told me about, and if you weren't, you'd know it alright. You're just wrestling with an admission. It'll come out sooner or later."

"And yet you're here with me."

"Sure. I don't look gift horses in the mouth. I knew the score all along. I don't try to steer the fates."

Tie that if you can, and I thought I knew women. I'll never think that again.

The next morning, earlier than I had any intention of getting up, I was awake and thrumming like a tight wire in anticipation of the following evening. There was a sickish, hurt feeling beneath my sternum, but it had to wait. I didn't have time to treat with it.

I ate the breakfast which Prett put before me (what that gal can't do to the lowly egg) and had my excitement detoured, because I sat there eating with her across the table not paying the proper attention to the robe she wore. It was one of mine that engulfed her that had a trick of opening at the wrong, or right places, at a moment's notice. This put off the departure for a while, but I finally deposited her at her place and raised my hand to stem what I thought was another session of mutual admiration, but it wasn't that.

"I talked to the lawyer yesterday."

"What did he say?"

"It was pitiful in a way. He can use me and he wants me the worst way, but it seems that old bag he married will have to approve me; and if the rest of his help is a sample of her approval, I don't have a chance."

"Well, run it out and see. If it doesn't work out, let me know."

"Thanks, Frank. 'Bye."

I lit a shuck down the Freeway and in no time I was striding into the Quality Market, inhaling smells that always intrigue me...those of a well bred grocery where the stock is what it should be.

Sam was calling off stock to Vincent...a short inventory or something. They do that occasionally when they anticipate a run on certain stock, or when a favorite salesman is due.

"Well, well," I began, sarcastically, "the purveyor of ptomaine at work over his cauldron. Sorry you're busy, because I had some adventure all cooked up. I think I'll take Sadie instead. She would probably be a lot better on this deal because she is smaller and not nearly as noisy."

"There are some cast-off herring in the garbage there," he said, easily. "Help yourself while I complete this check."

"What a thing to say," said Vincent, making a face. "He just sampled a new cask, Frank. Help yourself."

I picked out a succulent filet, and let the taste sensation ripple through my mouth and throat. After four of them, I said: "These herring haven't been in the ocean since you were a boy, Sam."

"You should have eaten the ones I offered you," he retorted. "They haven't been in the ocean since *you* were a boy."

I shut up after that and devoted myself to the herring, and spying a hunk of tough bread, yanked off a piece and tasted the contrast.

They were through in thirty minutes, during which time I wandered around tasting smoked dried beef, cheeses, Romano, Ricotta, Belpaese, Gorgonzola, and a few more I couldn't name.

"Now, little boy," said Sam, putting down his pencil, "before you run up a bill you can't pay, what fevers your infinitesimal brain?"

"Well, there's on tap for tonight something that is not entirely leg work. It involves … ," and I told him the whole layout as it involved Coniver.

When I got through, his eyes were no longer calm and mocking, but alive and bright. "Sol Well, this sounds like old times when we led the dear old C.D.D. through the muck and mire of Bougainville, where death did breathe smoke and flame upon our invincible backs. Tell me more."

"Well, I've promised Coniver that we'd be there ready for any eventuality. I told him to go there gassed up somewhat and raise all manners of hell. That should give Denkyn something of a shock."

"What shall we carry in the way of ordnance?"

"Do you still have that carbine?"

He closed one eye. "After shipping it back screw by screw, should anyone else have it?"

"And ammo?"

"And ammo. Moreover, I have six Triton blocks with seven second fuses … so it reads, a .45 automatic, also sent back screw by spring, a Nambu light machine gun, sent back with the blessings of Intelligence, a knee mortar with seventeen rounds of mortettes …"

"What's mortettes?"

"A coinage. Mortar ammo. I tire of dictionary English."

"So I thought. What, no eight inch coast artillery?"

"Well …" He frowned, then brightened. "I have the rotating band from an eight inch shell, if that'll help."

"I doubt that it will. What say you bring the carbine. There's a tree about twenty five yards south of the lodge, and that whole side of the living room is glass. It'll be a good point of vantage."

"Very good, so far. What else?"

I glanced at him closely. "No twitters?"

"Not a twit. Where will you be?"

"Well, I'll be under the house for a moment to see if their conversation is loud enough to record. Then I thought I'd hang around close and see what sort of spot I could pick for myself. I better stay away from that north window, in case you have to shoot, and miss."

He snorted like a steam shovel. "Me miss? Do you often miss your mouth? We don't want to kill Denkyn, do we?" Just like that … just wanted information.

"Look, you bloodthirsty guinea, we just want to save Coniver. Wing him if you have to shoot."

"Bloodthirsty?" A seismic chuckle shook him. "Son, I quit tying knots in my saber sash for Japs, and they hadn't done me a thing. People like Denkyn should earn their executioners a medal."

"Maybe so, but it ain't the law."

"Law. I spit on that sort of law. That's why you and me have to cough up a third of our earnings, and men like him manage to buy a tax official and get off easy."

"That is treason," I said, sanctimoniously.

" 'If that be treason,' to quote an Irish ancestor, Sir Gerald Micheal Patrick of Henry, 'make the most of it.' "

"Damn if you don't pop up with more high bred blood, Scotch and Irish."

"The Salvatos," he said, loftily, "are an intensely well bred family."

I nodded. "With all that, and Salvato. Famous old Irish name."

He shrugged. "Well, there was a soldier of fortune, name of Petrucci Alvarado Salvato, who led one of the squadrons of the ill-fated Spanish Armada, and you know what happened? They wrecked, and went ashore in Ireland, where they were welcomed and given E for effort, if not V for victory. The name was O'Salvato for years. We grew tired of the spelling and went back to the old one, which was given us by one of the early Venetian kings who leaned heavily on us for moral support and advice."

I sighed. From long experience, I knew this could go on like a streak of bad weather. "Look, I'll pick you up at three. I think we should get down there and case the place well before they arrive. Coniver says they usually get there about six and start drinking, then eat whenever the spirit moves them."

"Any dogs?"

A chill went over me. "That I don't know. I wish I did."

"In that case, I suppose I should take some fried liver and a silencer for the carbine."

"You got a silencer?"

"How else," he asked, sarcastically patient, "could I bring one?"

"Yeah. I didn't know those things could be silenced."

"To an ordnance expert like me it was a cinch, although I did get the idea from a Jap silencer I found on Bougainville."

"Well, shall I pick you up at three?"

"By all means. I'll be ready."

I turned to go, but stopped. "Look, neither of us can tell what this thing will amount to. Suppose you put a couple of those Triton blocks in your pocket and ... you never lost that knife did you?"

He grinned. "I still have my soul and my knife. After spending three years working on it, I would hardly lose it."

Riding back toward Houston, I thought of Sam and the knife. It had been hand-made by a Sea Bee ... the guys who could make or do anything from a piece of crosscut saw. The blade was ground sharp on both sides and was some seven inches long, coming to a point that always made me shudder. Sam could have been heard almost any time, day or night, with that interminable wheet, wheet, wheet, working that knife down until it could be bent like a Toledo blade, and I've shaved with many a blade duller than that knife. The handle was big and too heavy for me, having been poured and molded from lead then worked down to hand size. Sam used to claim he had his palm prints etched in it. Thing was, he used it for throwing and, with that heavy handle, it was lethal. No one seems to know where he learned to throw a knife, but I never saw anyone outside of a side show who could touch him and, when we were lost once in Guadal, that knife brought us out with a deadliness and lack of noise no bullet could rival. He never threw it with the mincing fencing-master air that most knife throwers use, but with a terrific short-armed swing that never failed to bury it right down to the hilt ... usually accompanied with a dull thud that was some indication of the horrible force with which it had been driven. Sam with a knife behind me, and I'm a brave hombre.

While I was home getting into dark blue slacks, dark blue T-shirt with long sleeves, and an old, blue corduroy coat to hide my gun, the phone rang.

"Mr. Barden?" It was Denkyn.

"Yap."

"What are you doing tonight?"

"Off. I'm dating a cricket. Cute, too."

"I'm afraid that will be impossible. I wish you to accompany me on a little trip."

"Sorry," I said, with deliberate emphasis. "When a-cricketing I go, business takes a back seat. Not interested."

"Has it occurred to you that you have done very little to earn a magnificent salary?"

"Well, I'll tell you. I've been interfered with. Three of my bosses are always wanting me to spy on the other two. Nevertheless, I was instrumental in seeing that Bramlett was well taken care of last evening."

"*What?*" It sure was near a scream for a big man.

"You heard me. The Rangers now have him."

"Why wasn't I informed?"

"Hell, I thought you knew everything. Don't I rate congratulations?"

There was a momentary silence during which time I could almost see him sweating and squirming.

"Well, of course. Indeed. A neat bit of work, Mr. Barden. Where did the Rangers take him?"

"To hell, I hope. The last time I saw them, they were cleaning the rack for him. I hope they get some life stories from him. I rather imagine he could write a good book."

"By the way, Mr. Barden. Do you know a man named Coniver?"

"Sure. Your chauffeur. How is Dicky, by the way?"

"I have discharged him."

"You have? Where is he?"

"I understand Nodd hired him."

"Well, they ought to cook up something nice in the way of a brew."

"That is abstruse. What do you mean?"

I sighed. People were always asking me what I meant. "I mean that it does seem funny that you, who once knew a man named

Coniver, should hire his daughter, sleep with her, hire his son … I don't suppose you slept with him, although Nodd might … then fire the son. Where is Dene?"

"She's fired, too, and how did you know I knew Coniver?"

"Mr. Denkyn, I know everything. What you should be concerned with is: How much will I tell?"

He sputtered, and I cut the connection. Someone might have seen me visiting Coniver. If so, then the old man's vision of him floating on the lake might not be silly at that, unless Sam and I could do something. Still, there were just two of us, and Denkyn sounded suspicious.

CHAPTER ELEVEN

We sat in the brush and sword grass a hundred yards back of Denkyn's lodge and watched the sun set.

"If you forgot the mosquito lotion," said Sam, "I shall shove your nose under the water and hold it there for a time that I confidently predict will be discommodious."

"I didn't forget. What about the stuff you were supposed to bring?"

"I never forget! You say you're afraid Denkyn suspects you of having traffic with Coniver?"

"He asked me point blank if I knew a man named Coniver. I said I did, his chauffeur. Then, like a fool, I let him know I did know of a Coniver and that he, Denkyn, had known him."

"I'm tempted to tread forcibly on your toes," said Sam, disgustedly. "Our luck now will be to rush headlong into an army of torpedoes ... gratefully furnished by one Antonio Charroni, who is somewhat irritated at the way you treated him and some of his most muscular henchmen the other night at his eatery."

"Oh, you've heard?"

"I heard the next day. He is somewhat baffled, and I think a little scared. In all the history of the Unione Sicilione, no man has ever conquered an entire roadhouse from boss to bouncers."

"I had help."

"So I thought. Calling in all the bouncers was probably your idea, since you always can think your way into ridiculous situations, then depend on the help to think you out."

"Why would he help Denkyn?"

"Sometimes I sorrow for you. Didn't you know that Denkyn put Antonio in business?"

"No, I didn't know it. I'm one of the central figures in this business, and I'm the last one to know about things like that."

"Did it ever occur to you that you have made some pretty good strides in this case, and yet about all you've done has been to bring pretty girls to your den, and ride back and forth from Houston to Dickinson?"

"All things come to those who wait. There's one thing you don't know."

"Doubtful, but what?"

"Bramlett is in custody."

He chuckled. "Yes, rammed from behind by Roller Lester while trying to blast you. Why else would you be driving a rented car? Yours is being repaired."

"Look, the car we came here in is just like mine, color and everything. How ... ?"

"And has a sticker on the windshield that says: 'This is your car for as long as you want it. Treat it like yours, Bradford U Drive It Company.' "

I think I flushed a little, because he said: "You'd never make a detective, son. You miss obvious things."

It was now dusk, and as the light died, I got restless. I looked at my watch. Seven-fifteen. They were late, and I liked that not at all.

"I," said Sam, also looking at his watch, "feel a distinctly uncomfortable twitter."

"You do? Why?"

He shrugged. "Your talkativeness for one thing. Denkyn is an old and experienced operator; why do you suppose he ever hired you in the first place?"

"That, I'd like to know. It was his idea."

"Maybe he had something cooked up for you, but your lack of cooperation made him change his plans."

"I thought of that. Like tonight. He wanted me along."

"How chummy! I suppose he wanted you to drive bamboo splinters beneath Coniver's nails and set fire to them."

"He wanted me for no good, you can bet. I don't think we were followed."

"If he had a lookout, there'd be no need for following. As I see it, he only knows that you have some knowledge of Coniver. He could hardly know that you promised to be here tonight."

I pondered a moment. "We did come in pretty openly. The car is hidden well enough, but if he had a lookout, we've been spotted."

"I," said Sam, magnificently, "have a destiny. It is not in the books that I shall be taken by an example of that strata of our society which feels that the rules, such as they are, have all been waived in favor of Their Highnesses."

As it grew darker, Salvato began aiming the carbine at distant objects, muttering range data to himself in an undertone. "Range twelve hundred, elevation dead-on with adjustment, wind quartering at seven miles an hour."

"With that popgun, any range over a hundred yards is sheer optimism," I opined.

"Spoken like a tyro. Tom Jones smote me lovingly on the back at La Jolla … "E" Range it was, and I had just made a possible, standing, off-hand at a thousand yards."

"That was with an '03."

He shrugged. "This isn't a bad weapon, using Kentucky windage, holding over, and stuff."

"Just the same, it ain't a 105 … Is that a Rolls coming around that turn?"

"It is. Pride of merry England on wheels. Is that Denkyn's buggy?"

I unslung a pair of 8 X 50s and took a look. "That's him, and he lied. That's Dicky driving. Why do you suppose he told me Dicky had been fired?"

"There are other things that concern us more. Is Coniver on the back seat?"

"No. That must be Coniver following in the Ford."

I let dark fall like a blanket before creeping toward the house. Sam stayed where he was, and would reach his tree ten minutes after I had time to get under the house.

After a great deal of crawling and some low aping, I got to a growth of brush not far from the corner of the house, but someone had turned on a light in the bathroom, and it sent out a finger of light right athwart the path I wanted to take to the house, so I had to wait. The light went off after five minutes and I walked boldly to the back and ducked under the house, making my way to the spot where I had stashed the recorder gismo. I reached up and snapped the switch with a pop that sounded like a small firecracker. It had been heard above, too.

I heard Denkyn's voice say: "What the hell was that?"

Another voice, that I took to be Coniver, said: "I didn't hear anything."

Then Dicky's voice: "You got bad ears, you creaking old bastard. You always did have."

Coniver's reply was heated. "What did I ever do to you, Dicky? I tried to treat you like a son, and you always bit the hand."

Denkyn's laugh was deep and rich. "That's what you get for marrying a woman whose son had already done two stretches in reform school, Doug. Your own progeny is satisfactory, isn't it?"

"You mean Danessa? She's a fine girl."

"And you better treat her right, too," grumbled Dicky, "else I'll be coming to see you."

"Who," asked Coniver, not relishing the subject, "were those other four men who got out down the road?" You can imagine how my neck crawled at that.

"None of your business, Doug. I rather have an idea you and Barden have been putting your heads together. He admitted he knew you."

"I know no man by that name," said Coniver, easily. "I need a drink."

"Get him a drink, Dicky."

"Let him get his own drinks. I ain't no serving maid."

"There's plenty in the kitchen, Doug. You'd better bring the bottle in here. You may need it." There were footsteps that went to the kitchen and came back.

"Maybe we'll both need it, you leather-faced idiot."

I almost busted a gusset wanting to laugh at the dead, pregnant silence that followed his cheerful curse.

"What did you say, Doug?" That was Denkyn, and I could tell he had gotten to his feet.

"You heard me … that is, unless your ears are really what they look like."

"And what do they look like?" soft and deadly … menacing.

"Mildewed acorns on a frosty morning." I'd have to get out of here. I wouldn't be able to stand any more.

There was the sound of a furious oath, a blow, a thud, and the tinkle of window glass, followed closely by a bellow of pain from Denkyn.

"Dicky … get out there … wait …" Sulphurous language, delivered in a high-pitched roar, anguished and unbelieving.

"Get …"

"What the hell's the matter with you?" asked Dickie, plainly thunderstruck.

"I'm shot … wounded …"

"Where?"

"My back, you fool!" There was a slither of cloth, and Dicky chuckled. "It ain't much. Just a crease."

"Not *much!* You blasted idiot, don't you realize I've been shot! Look at the window!" Sounds of inspection.

"Then I think we're fools, standing here in the light."

"There was a click, and the lights went off. For a while, there was no sound but dry chuckles from Coniver.

"That'll show you, you creep," said Coniver. "Just touch me again, and this whole place will go down around your ears."

"Coniver," said Denkyn, malignantly, "I'll get you for this."

I left after that and made my way to the tree, where Sam roosted uncomfortably in the foliage. "Better come down, now," I whispered. "They've turned out the lights. There's four men around some place, too."

"Night as black as Coaly's tail, too," he grumbled, as he came down, "and in an hour the moon'll be up. Then we'll have to turn into weasels."

We went back to the lodge and tried to peer inside... carefully, of course, but we couldn't see a thing.

"I'm going under again," I whispered. "I might hear something."

I did. Coniver was chortling in a high, hysterical voice. "Going to put the screw on me, were you? Well, why don't you go ahead. I've got allies..." He lit into a storm of cursing to which Denkyn replied in kind, but even with the lights out, the latter was afraid to do anything.

That went on for some time, with both of them drinking, and I knew it would only be a matter of time before Denkyn's reinforcements came into the play... I still didn't know how. I scrambled back where I had left Sam, crawled out from under the house, and straightened up right by a guy I didn't know from Adam. Sam was gone, and my stomach felt miserable with a gun in the middle of it.

"Inside, neighbor," hissed a voice.

I knew better than to resist at this point, so I went, wondering with a sinking feeling what had happened to Salvato, the Great. There were supposed to be three more, but unless they were pretty good, they'd need three more than that to keep him corralled. With that thought to strengthen me, I went on in as I was ordered.

"Who's there?" asked Dicky.

"Paul," said my guard. "I got one of 'em."

It had finally occurred to them to pull the curtains and, as I was pushed in, the lights went on. Coniver went white, but a wink from me bucked him up. Denkyn smiled thinly, although his face was pale and the knot on his back was crimson in spots. He had packed the scratch with a towel.

"My tried and trusted employee," he said, acting like a movie villain.

"I'll take care of him," said Dicky, stepping forward and letting me have one under the ear. I went down because staying upright would have meant more of the same, and I didn't feel brave right then.

"Get up," he ground out, savagely. "I owe you a couple on account."

"You always were a coward," said Coniver, with surprising courage. "Tell that yegg to put away his gun and see how long you'd last."

Dicky walked over to the older man. "Your grey hairs don't mean a thing to me, old man."

"Of course not, except that I probably couldn't give you much of a fight."

He slapped Coniver hard, then let out a bellow, spun around, and fell to the floor. "Down ... somebody left a curtain cracked!"

No one did anything for a moment, watching Dicky tear open his shirt, exposing the raw, red furrow across his stomach; then there was a concerted dive for the only window whose curtain was cracked. On the floor lay a little scattering of glass glittering in the light.

From outside there came a scuffling and a shriek that could have come only from a man. A hoarse, tortured scream like a horse in a fire.

We all tensed, and for a while, no one spoke; then there came a tap on the door.

"Who's there?" yelled Dicky.

"Turk. I got the last one."

How had they done it? I twisted around to see Turk…a thick-chested, currant-eyed thug I didn't know, dragging Salvato by one arm. The back of his head was a mass of blood and matted hair.

"Bring him in, bring him in," chortled Denkyn. "Now that the house is full, we can proceed."

Turk dragged Sam over and propped him against the wall near me, then he and Paul, whom I now recognized as the last two bouncers of that night club fracas, sat opposite us and held us at the point of snub-nosed revolvers.

"Where's Ed and Smalley?" asked Denkyn.

"Out there," said Turk. "I stayed back 'cause I thought they could handle him, but he just popped Ed's arm like a cane and Ed passed out. Smalley looks like his neck is busted. I snuck up when I seen that, and sapped him. I didn't fool around outside, 'cause somebody might hear."

Denkyn nodded easily, and seemed to forget about his wound. "Well, I think all our troubles are right here in the same room, and may be disposed of neatly and without any difficulty." He turned to Coniver. "Now I see where your Dutch courage came from. Like to continue on the same lines?"

Coniver swallowed noisily, and said nothing.

Denkyn nodded with satisfaction. "So I thought. However, Doug, I'm afraid your usefulness is at an end…"

"A long time ago," said Dicky, holding his stomach with a bloody hand, "a long time ago."

"Yes," Denkyn continued, turning to me. "You are too inquisitive, Mr. Barden…and too impertinent."

"A lot too impertinent," said Dicky, looking at me with a savage gleam in his eyes.

"Who is your friend?" asked Denkyn.

For some reason, I started to tell a lie about Sam, then quite inexplicably changed my mind.

"He's Samuel J. Salvato, of Dickinson, Texas. I think maybe some of you have heard of him. One thing, sure: I know a couple who *will* hear from him."

Turk and Paul tightened up like a couple of kids who had seen a snake, but Denkyn only smiled. "Well, he'll have to be quite the man to do anything... from the bottom of the lake."

Coniver shriveled up, then straightened and shook himself. At last his courage shook off support, and he stood alone. And I do mean alone.

Turk stood up slowly and looked at Denkyn. "Look, didn't nobody mention nuthin' to me about no killin'. I ain't no killer, and if that's Salvato..." He took a quick look at the silent figure beside me and almost shivered. "No, sir. You can count me out."

"You cowardly swine," snarled Denkyn. "Charroni told you to take orders from me!"

"He sure did," said Paul, finding his voice, "but he didn't say nuthin' about no killin'."

"For once, you're showing some sense," I said. "Salvato was once a Ranger. Bramlett killed a man who was a Ranger, and he's all ready to stretch hemp right now."

Dicky aimed a foot at me, which I partly dodged, but the toe caught my cheek and banged my head off the wall, filling the air with stars. "You'll be called on. Keep quiet till you are."

So the impasse had arrived, with Paul and Turk glaring at Denkyn, and being glared at in return.

Dicky reached for his gun, but Paul's was out and lined up with his belly button before he could get his hand on it.

"Beat it, Turk," said Paul, grimly. "I'll be right behind you. We stand to take the rap for this batty bunch the way it's lined up."

"Right," said Turk, and moved fast for the door.

When they had gone, Denkyn smiled. "This makes fewer to know. Better, probably."

I laughed, but I sure didn't feel like it. "And two more witnesses at your trial, but not for your side."

Denkyn's grin widened. "Don't be silly. They can be handled. I don't think they'll talk."

"Handled like you figure on handling us?"

"Precisely. Doug, it is a pity you couldn't see fit to play ball with me in this. You'll be the means of making a criminal of me. Aren't you ashamed?"

"No," said Coniver, flatly. His courage was still doing all right. "You were born a dog, Denkyn. You'll die a dog. There's little choice between a carrion-eating dog and a murdering dog."

Dicky's slap knocked the old man out of the chair, but it didn't make him quail. He sat up on the floor and glared defiantly.

Denkyn turned to me. "Barden, I had a different role for you tonight, but either you're more clever than I supposed, or you're lucky. I knew I'd have use for you, but I didn't count on you becoming a nuisance before I was ready. A pity. If you'd listened to reason."

"What was for me, tonight?"

"A simple matter of a man shot, a switched gun, and the police notified and given a story to fit. We had it all planned, but you had a 'date' tonight. No matter. I think it can be arranged so the murder ..." He stopped and beamed. "Why not? A pity I didn't think of this before the other two left. Do you think you could find them, Dicky?"

"I don't know," said Dicky, stolidly. "I'll go to my grave not knowing."

Denkyn shrugged. Dicky didn't relish going after two toughs in the dark.

"Yes," continued the former. "It will be perfect. Coniver and Barden got in an argument. We were here and quieted them. We left, making Coniver leave ahead of us, but evidently he came back. His car will be found. Mr. Salvato, utterly free of interest in the argument or culpability, got in the way of a bullet from Coniver's gun." He smiled widely. "Capital idea, don't you think, Barden?"

"Flawless," I agreed, thinking of the recorder under the house. Well, I couldn't do much, so I might as well make it as good as I could. "Tell me, Denkyn, since I'll never be able to use the information, who killed Wenken? Bramlett?"

Denkyn shook his head. "I'm not sure. He says he didn't. I frankly don't know. I had plans of my own for Wenken, but they weren't needed. You were to play a part in that, too, Barden. You would have earned your money alright."

He began pacing up and down, rubbing his chin reflectively. "Yes, and Nodd, too. I had plans for him, involving you, but now I'll have to change them. Barden, neither Wenken or Nodd appreciated the wonders money could buy. What use was it to them? Why shouldn't I have it all? Now Dicky there, a diamond in the rough, knows more about it than both of them put together. Money..." He stopped, faced me, and smacked his lips. "Barden, you never really knew the power of money, did you? Tons of it, buying things, working for you, beautiful women with white, soft flesh, clinging to you, begging you to accept their favors, exposing their most delectable areas to your caresses, capitulating at your whim and begging for more."

A mad light seemed to creep into his eyes. "Money... green and fresh and crisp. To build empires, move counties, and voters at your will. How does this sound to you, Barden: Thaddeus Hannibal Denkyn, President of the United States?"

At that precise moment I *knew*. Denkyn was a madman. A clever, calculating, diabolical madman with a madman's utter disregard for either an act or the consequences of it, and unless something happened, we'd lay there and grow cold and stiff on the floor of that lodge and his story, although recorded differently on the wire, might go through unchallenged. After all, he was a big man, and I had done a maidenly job of hiding the recorder. It might never be found.

Dicky sat where Coniver had been, and watched his employer through expressionless eyes. If he was impatient, he didn't show it.

"Money," Denkyn was saying, continuing his pacing, "can buy anything man has to deal with, Mr. Barden. It can buy other men, it can buy influence, it can buy government agencies, it can influence the course of history, and the man who has it as I shall have it is a king who needs no crown, a king who enjoys all of the privileges and none of the responsibilities. What happened to the wealthy after the first World War? Krupp, Farben, and the rest of them? Money has no country, Mr. Barden. It is the true internationalizer. World War Two has been fought, but already wealth in conquered countries is being courted by wealth in Britain and this country. They will not allow it to die, because they would be sealing their own doom. No matter who rides out the third World War, wealth will be ahead of all. It is the true nobility and it watches out after its own, no matter things like countries, idiotic patriotism, or loyalty to this or that tenet. Wealth is loyal to wealth, always has been and always will be. It is the international royal family and it will look out after its own. Mark..."

Never in all my born days did I ever see a big man move with such speed. Sam came up off that floor like a striking rattler and sank one, shattering right to Denkyn's jaw and, completing the swoop, landed one on the stupefied Dicky before he could even snatch for the gun that lay on his knees. Down they went, the chair splintering to matchwood beneath that berserk onslaught and, though Dicky was thewed like a bull, he was a babe.

Catching him in the shirt, Sam banged his head once on the floor with such force that dust arose from the cracks.

Denkyn lay on the floor near me, his head at a peculiar angle which I started to investigate. Then I turned my eyes to Dicky, from whose prone carcass Sam was rising, his normally calm, brown eyes swirls of flecked yellow flame.

"The logical moment arrived," he said casually, brushing himself off.

"And, sir," said Coniver, shaking as though in the grip of ague, "I never saw a moment pounced upon with more devastating effect. Allow me to congratulate you."

Sam bowed choppily and walked to the phone where, after some back chat from the operator, he located Roller's Ranger station.

"Roller, this is Sam Salvato ... yes. Better come out to Poule D'eau at once. There are some collections you might like to make ... plus interest."

"I told Roller we were going before I left," I said, realizing that I still sat on the floor and getting up as though it was hot.

"Then what's he doing still at the office?"

"Well ..." I stopped and looked, I'm sure, quite foolish. "I think I told him I'd contact him by ten and, if I didn't, he'd know trouble was afoot."

Sam grunted and glanced at Dicky. "You sure allowed plenty of time. It is just twenty till ten, and it would have taken him an hour at the very least to get here. We could have been fish bait by then."

"When did you come to?" I asked.

"About the time Paul and Turk decided that the name Salvato was not to be trifled with."

"Your name struck terror to their hearts," said Coniver, dramatically.

"They struck terror to mine, too," admitted Sam, feeling the gash in the back of his head. "I'll often wonder how a man as big as Turk ever sneaked up behind me."

I went outside, but if Ed's arm was busted and ditto for Smalley's neck, they had had help getting away. They were nowhere to be seen. I went back and reported, bringing in Sam's carbine.

"They blew, so your chop must have missed the target."

Coniver, who was bending over Denkyn, looked up, his face white and drawn. "I ... er, think we have a fatality here."

JOHN B. THOMPSON

"Tough," I said, unsympathetically.

"Rough," said Sam.

Dicky sat up and was promptly pushed back to the floor by Sam's foot. "Frank, look around in the kitchen and see if you can find a light cord or something we can tie this lug up with. Some thin, waxed cord like fishing line will do fine. I've been wanting..."

"I know. You want to try that tie method you learned from Lt. Kabaguchi."

"Exactly."

I found some thin silk stuff on a reel in the kitchen ... belonging to someone's rod, and Sam did the job while Dicky looked at him as though he weren't seeing right. When the job was finished, Dicky gave a herculean wrench and bawled like a branded steer.

"You ruined my fingers," he grated, half sobbing from pain.

"*You* ruined them," corrected Sam, instructively. "You've probably cut off circulation and some M.D. will have to amputate them."

Dicky glared hatefully, and strained his neck trying to see what damage had been done.

Next day, after all the details had been taken care of by the local authorities under the watchful eye of Roller Lester, he had me cornered in his Dad's house not too far from Denkyn's place in River Oaks.

"Now look," he said, offensively sarcastic, "are you and Sam going to insist that he broke Denkyn's neck with his fist, or will you break down and tell the truth for a change?"

"You have the truth, and that's all I can tell you. You have the delecti corpuscle, or whatever it is called, plus a recorded admission that he was about to do us in for good and all. What else do you want?"

CHAPTER TWELVE

Old Dr. Lester, still tall and straight after thirty years of administering to the sick, cackled rustily and stroked the sparse, white hair on his head. "It isn't unusual for a man to kill another with his fists. Even with boxing gloves on it happens. I recall once … let's see. Yes. Hadley Wenken's father killed a man once with his fist. Was sitting on a horse when he did it, too. Both of them were moving toward each other when it happened, which probably explained old Ab's compound fracture of the forearm. It was a sight."

"Sam," I pointed out, "will shift back and forth from two-fifty to two-seventy. He's as agile as a cat and as strong as a wild Brahma. He's usually mild, but when he gets stirred up, he's a killer. He came off that floor like a shot out of a gun, and that blow came all the way from the canals of Venice. If you'd have seen and heard it, you wouldn't wonder that it broke Denkyn's neck."

"A blow of that sort," explained Dr. Lester, "acts much like the knot on a hangman's rope. The knuckles, catching the angle of the jaw with terrific force, backed by considerable weight, simply tilts the cervical vertebrae to such an extent that a fracture and consequent damage to the spinal cord results. Done slowly, the musculature of the neck would have had time to tense, thereby taking up most of the force. There was no time for this saving reaction to assert itself."

"That's pretty plain," I said, "to me."

Roller roughed up his hair and shook his head. "Well, maybe so. Mind you, I'm not bothered that the man's dead. He was a hazard and a lunatic. It just don't seem like a man, not even Salvato, could snap a man's neck like a stalk of sugar cane."

"That gadget did a good job of recording," I said.

He nodded. "They're new and haven't been tried too much, but they seem to have promise. You had it well located, too. That helped."

"There won't be any trouble about Coniver, will there?"

"No. He didn't come out by name on the wire. We just don't know who he is."

"If Dicky doesn't peach."

"I think Dicky'll be good. There are any number of reasons, but as far as I'm concerned, Wenken's killer is still at large."

"That's right. What did you get out of Bramlett?"

"Not a word. He said you were after him on that lease deal, and he was taking the easiest way to get out from under. I think there's a lot more to that than meets the eye. Murder is still a fairly serious matter in Texas. Bramlett's alibi stands up for the time of the murder."

I left soon afterward and drove slowly home, pounding my head to bits, trying to find some answer to the murder business. Denkyn had wanted to be rid of Wenken and Nodd...that must be it. Denkyn. Well, we'd never know.

Somehow I didn't want to go home. I thought of that house all quiet and alone and shivered with revulsion. Still, if this day was anything like others recently, I'd have company soon.

Marlo might get over her mad and call. The thought chased my appetite that had begun to growl, and down I went into the confused glooms. Did I love her? If not, why couldn't I answer the question? Seeing where this was taking me, I shied away from it and tried to think about the murder again, but I didn't have any luck. The thought struck me that I still hadn't done anything about the kid's dress, so I went on home and spoke to

Miss McCausland, a husky spinster who knew everything about women's clothes.

"What's she like?" she blared, hurting my ear.

"She's a cute brunette about five two or three, saucy, and with a grown-up tendency."

"How old is she?"

"Oh ... sixteen or seventeen."

"My God, Frank, you're taking them on pretty young, aren't you?"

"Look," I yelled, getting hot in the face, "I'm trying to do the kid a favor. Her dad has no money and she wants to go to the Senior Prom."

"Ha, ha, ha," she laughed. "That's a new angle you're stuck with, but if you say so, I'll follow directions to the letter and send you the bill."

"Yeah ... do that, and keep it under your hat."

"I'm a very discreet lady who knows more than she tells."

"I'm sure! G'bye."

I went to the bar, and though it wasn't quite lunch time, I touched up the rum bottle and went back to the couch, where I sat only to be bounced up by the phone.

"Hey, Frank ... Brown."

"What's up?"

"I found the plane for you."

"You did ... where?"

"Private field about two miles past the southern tip of Lake Poule D'eau. I saw the strip, and since I was flying pretty low, I caught the bright red nose even though it was under a T shed. I was flying my own crate, so I set her down and investigated. No one was around, but the nose had been painted red, over the green, then green again. Not too good a job."

"Did you spot the yellow streamers?"

"They've been removed, but there were a few threads of lint still."

"Hey, you didn't disturb that lint, did you?"

"No, sir. I didn't touch the thing. There were signs that the numbers had been taped out with masking tape or something like it."

"You get the number?"

"Yeah. It's Denkyn's plane."

I slumped, and told him in a tired voice what had happened the night before. "So," I wound up, "I guess that finishes the case."

"Looks that way. Sorry I didn't find it sooner."

"Forget it. Say, what'll you do for a living now?"

"Guess what … the old man left me the plane. With a crate like that, I can get more top flight charter jobs than I can fill. I'm in clover, boy. Wenken was a man among men."

I called Roller and we agreed that the murder business was fini, then I spent fifteen minutes putting the drink down and, true to my previous conviction, I had company.

A blue convertible slid to a stop, and Dene Coniver jumped out and sprinted up the walk. I let her in, only to have her climb me like a squirrel. Three minutes later I was reeling from the impact of her lips backed up by a brand of seductiveness that was all her own, springing from the way she handled herself, the manner in which she tried to eat me alive, and the pressure of her breasts pricking their presence through my shirt like knitting needles.

"I'm so glad it's all over," she said. "Now we can see more of each other."

"That would be a fancy idea," I said, giving her the eye. "Right now you seem pretty well covered."

"Sit down, Frank."

I sat, and was happy I did. She was slow and her smile was warm; the corners of her mouth quirked spasmodically as she flounced about in her linen dress.

She was a fragrant bundle of womanhood; small, piquant, and the soft attractions of her body were now in second place to the gymnastics which sprang from a nature that demanded its due and was determined to get it.

Three hours later, the phone roused us from a placid, thoughtless repose which made me a shade touchy until I found out who it was.

"Frank, I'm really sorry about the other night. I had no reason to run out on you like that."

"I think I understand," I said, guardedly.

Her sob came over the phone, freighting an outsized burden of loneliness. "Then ..."

"Sure. When?"

"Will you let me buy you a dinner at Lippman's tonight, in the private dining room?"

"Sure, kid. Same time?"

"Yes. That'll be fine. See you there."

I hung up and went back to the bedroom, where Dene lay curled up on the bed like a small, self-satisfied cat.

"Who was that?"

"That was Sam Salvato. He and I have to clean up the case for Roller tonight." The lie came out easily.

She pouted. "I don't want to go home."

"What'll you do now that Denkyn is dead?"

"I have to help the administrator get things in order. I'll be there for a month, at least. Frank, don't wait for me next time ... call me."

"Sure ... sure. I'll have more time, now."

"Frank, I'm so glad you've given up chasing murderers. You make a better lover than you do a detective. I felt that Denkyn was the man all along."

That night at Lippman's, Marlo wasn't a mere woman, she was a sylph done out in a pale lavender jersey thing that nearly gave me heart failure the way it fit. The sleeves were long and the buttons all the way down the front looked like steel balls lacquered with purple. Her hair had been brushed until it shone like metal, and yet it had a casually nonchalant arrangement that didn't look contrived. Her face was smooth as peach down, and so perfectly made up that you couldn't see any paint except her lipstick. The rest of her face was its usual, creamy tan, and her eyes had a sparkle that spelled a couple before dinner. I put it into words.

"Looks like you're ahead of me."

"Only one. Does it show?"

"Not a lot. You're sparkling like a Christmas tree."

"I feel fine, Frank." Her face fell a little. "It hasn't been easy the last day or so."

"Look, kid, why do you build fires under yourself like that? You had me in a corner the other night and about things of that sort I don't go leaping blindly. I don't want to hurt you."

"Oh...don't I know that? I don't know why I did it." Her voice sank lower. "Frank, I'm so lonely."

"I still don't get it. You could be surrounded ten deep in good, solid, eager males. All ready to bring home their paycheck to you."

She shook her head. "I'm one of those people who can be lonely in a crowd. I've got to know that I'm something special to people."

"I thought I made it plain that you were special to me."

"You did, and that's why I'm with you now. That's why I feel safe and comfortable and...home."

"That's very sweet," I said, softly.

"Oh...don't speak like that. I'm all ready to melt away again." Her lips trembled, but she forced them to behave.

"What about the future, Marlo?"

She went tight all over. "Please don't ask me that. It's the one thing I don't want to think of. I'm never going back to the ranch..." Her face twisted with unbearable anguish, "...alone."

All right, Barden, it's up to you. The iron's hot. Nope, I didn't want it like that. There was still that scene at my house with me standing in the doorway, sleepy, stupid, and as dull as a monastery. That had made an impression, and until I could do something to erase it...

We drank several drinks, then ate...flounder again, at Marlo's request. Then we had a few more and left.

"Where do you want to go?" I asked. "Movie, clubbing..."

"No..." She looked in my eyes for a long four seconds. "Frank, I liked your house. Take me there and talk to me."

I nodded and looked around for a shadow, something I should have done that other night. I knew there would be none, but I had made up my mind to keep a lookout, anyhow.

At the house, I turned on an indirect lighting arrangement I had put in special for special occasions. It cast a glow without shadows and mingled several colors in such a way that Marlo looked like something out of a pipe dream. It brought out her rich, ripe coloring, yet it subdued and blended her beauty in such a way as to render it mistily suggestive rather than blatantly assertive. I made drinks and we toasted each other silently, a silence that continued until it became slightly uncomfortable.

"What was it you wanted to talk about?" I asked. "Anything in particular?"

"No..." Her voice was rich and feather soft, seeming to gather atmosphere from the gentle illumination of the room.

She toyed with the glass for a moment, the pressure building up and telegraphing its presence through her increased respiration and the pink flush that rose beneath the tan. "Frank, why is love something that has to be thought out and decided upon. I always thought of it as something that your emotions decided for you, something you couldn't avoid."

"I think you have a very vague conception of it, Marlo. Something foolishly romantic, as you said the other night. Love as a *something* should have a rather solid definition as a basis from which to work, in the event you are buried under some emotion which might resemble it, but is not it, really."

"I don't follow you."

I sat beside her, putting my glass on the coffee table. "I don't follow me too well myself. What I'm trying to say is this: Know what love *is* unless you want to be fooled every time you get over-heated in the pants."

She flushed deeper. "That was a little rugged, but I think I know what you mean. I wasn't in love with Harold … just physi-cal attraction."

"Not exactly. Love is physical attraction. The other things we are in the habit of plastering love with, spiritual quality, spiritual compatibility … that sort of attraction doesn't need the physical. It could as easily occur with a woman as with a man, a brother, a sister … anyone. After it is all hashed out, love boils down to one thing … physical attraction. Otherwise, there would be any number of great loves between people of the same sex … without there being any question of perversion. Through history there has been all sorts of drivel written about love, but no matter how ethereal and spiritual they tried to make it, there was always a man and woman involved."

"I think I see." There was a ponderous slowness about the sentence as though, by grabs, she *did* see. Her eyes were slated into sightlessness as the wheels of her mind moved, and the pic-ture was a little shaking.

She handed me the glass. "Fix me a drink, Frank … a power-ful one. I want it to strike me right out of myself. I want to climb the wall and see what you've told me. Oh, Frank, you're so *right*."

Animation sparked in her eyes and her teeth gleamed in a whole-hearted upsurge of spirits.

That gal, I told myself, is a bit of all right. Make a point and she's ready to see it. Not only see it, but allow it to impress. A sheet of chill flew like lightning up my back, and as I poured the drink, my hands trembled. I doubled hers and tripled my own. If she thought she needed a heavy one, I needed one twice as heavy.

She drank slowly, not like a person anxious to get numb ... in fact, she didn't seem to want to get numb. She had thinking to do. She caressed the cold glass with a long forefinger, saying nothing for a long time. She smiled and raised her eyes to mine. They were as deep as the ocean and as soft as pansy petals. She put the drink down and slid over close to me.

"Will you kiss me, Frank ... show me?"

I kissed her, but I'm afraid it was me who got shown. A curling, backlashing shock rippled through me at the butterfly touch of her lips, the tremulous quiver, and the long deep inhalation.

She was hard at first, and taut with the novelty of her first kiss ... of this sort at any rate. A frown leaped across her forehead and was erased instantly. As it fled, there was an all over softening, a bodily capitulation that traveled over her like the throwing of a switch. Gradually I drew her closer with both arms about her, her own hands lying placidly on my shoulders ... that is, until nature working her wonders loosened the muscles in her jaw and her mouth came hesitantly open. A clonic agitation jerked through her for a moment, then her arms went around my neck and a sound murmured deep within her.

She rose to one knee and forced me back against the couch, where her mouth seemed to change into a magic, dew-laden flower, intent upon devouring whatever it touched. It lasted long and when, with a shuddering sigh she sank back to the couch, she was spent. Her eyes were damp and enormous in the weird light as she touched her mouth with the back of her hand.

"Frank ..." It was a whisper, hardly a word at all. "I ... think ... I know ... now."

I let my hand slide over the shimmering waves of her hair. "Only partly, darling ... only partly."

She pushed up close and her face was a little distorted with the agonized earnestness of her heart. "Teach me, Frank ... please. Teach me slowly and gently. Be kind to me and don't hurt me." I drew her across my lap and gave her a long, affectionate kiss that

I gradually changed into something heated and passionate. I held her close, feeding my bloodstream on the new heat of her body.

I kissed her chin, her neck, then retraced the path to her lips again. Her reaction was so strong that I had to hold her tightly, and she was as strong as a man. My lips on hers quieted her momentarily, but her body was iron hard now, tensed. Her back went into retraction, but not far enough, then bowed itself into reverse.

She gasped, then started weeping and massaging her face on my chest, but her arms were like the grip of death. Neither man nor machine could have parted us then.

Some time later she revived, and began to weep all over again. Kissing my face and neck and shaking her head in an agony of remorse.

"I knew...somewhere back there that I couldn't stop you. Why...why didn't you stop us, Frank? I'm weak and horrible and you should hate me with all your heart and never speak to me again because I'm like all the rest of them and weak and horrible..."

I got up and, catching her roughly in my arms, I kissed her so hard I could hear her whimper with pain.

"Shut up," I said hoarsely, as I withdrew enough to speak. Her eyes were wide with...not fright, but that look of a woman when a man has established his position without question.

"Now," I said, cuttingly, "let's have an end of that bunk. I love you. Your ideas are screwy. No man could love a woman more than I love you. Tomorrow you'll go back to the ranch, invite friends and do whatever is necessary to do for whatever sort of wedding you want. In the meantime... *Stand up, Marlo.*"

She stood, shyly, pinked all over in one gigantic blush, but not without pride in possession of a magnificent body. It was like a shaft carved with the most exquisite art in pink jade with strong tan overtones. I got up, too, squared my shoulders, drew my muscles into etched definition, then drew her slowly to me.

She shivered as though chilled in a cold draft as we touched. I caught her close and tilted her head back by catching a handful of her hair. She whimpered a little from the pain that was ecstasy.

"In the meantime, you'll make love to me such as no man has ever known, or shall ever know again." She did! She needed no teaching, only a releasing, and Mother Eve, who has through all the thousands of years handed down knowledge, quite outdid herself in the endowment of Marlo.

CHAPTER THIRTEEN

Sam Salvato lighted one of his brown cigarettes and leaned back. "So you're going to get married?"

"Yeah. Soon."

"And, of course, I'll be best man."

"Second best."

"That I could have skipped. It is buried in the moss of ages."

"Okay. Do without it."

I brought him up to date—even to my last roll with Dene.

"So the murder of Wenken goes unsolved, and you marry the daughter. Neat."

"The murder is solved."

"Denkyn, eh?" He gave a ponderous shrug, hesitated, then grew taut. *"Nuts."*

"What?"

"I said, nuts. I had a twitter then that nearly knocked me over."

"Let 'er twitter. We're satisfied."

He shook his senatorial head. "Not me... Just a minute." He dialed a number and, as he waited for an answer, asked: "Did you say the plane had been found?"

"Yes. Brown found it. It was registered in Denkyn's name."

"Hello ..." He grinned and pitched up an eyebrow. "Er ... may I speak to Mr. Nodd? Ummm, what is a chick like that doing answering Nodd's phone?" He straightened sharply and bent over.

"This Nodd?" He sounded like a mugg, not Salvato. "Nemmine who dis is. Dat plane wid de new paint. It's been found. T'ought you might like to know." He hung up and leaped to his feet. "You know the way to that field?"

"No."

"Then call Brown and find out ... fast."

I had to try two airports and his house before I finally found him and got directions. All the time Sam was fretting like a five year old waiting for Santa Claus, because he thought he had fouled the deal by calling before we knew how to get there.

Sam has a Lincoln Continental that he bought second hand, and some cousin of his did all sorts of queer things to it. We were flying low when a motorcycle cop pulled out of a driveway after us just as we were getting on the road to Lake Poule D'eau. We lost him in the first ten miles because the road was so corduroyed he'd have been beaten to pieces by the seat of his motor if he had followed us at our speed.

We found the strip without much trouble, since it was on a side road that turned off about a mile past Denkyn's lodge.

We hid the car behind the hangar and sat with our backs to it, waiting. The idea that yellow old Nodd could have made himself up to look as big as Bramlett or Denkyn didn't seem within the realm of possibility, but right now I was feeling a little too chagrined to worry about that.

We didn't have long to wait ... about fifteen minutes in fact, when we heard the brakes of a car squeal and the sound of rubber cutting grass.

"Hold it," said Sam, as I made ready to sprint around the corner of the house with my gun in hand.

"Why?"

"And give them a chance to say they were just looking?"

"Oh!"

"Yeah."

We could hear the starter of the Cessna grinding, and soon the motor sounded off. There was not warm-up time and, as the pilot gave the ship the gun, Sam grabbed my arm. "Now!"

We leaped around the corner of the little T hangar just as the plane came blasting out. She saw us, and we saw her, but to say who was the more surprised would be hard to say.

It was Dene, and the look on her face when she saw us was something. It didn't look much like her any more.

The plane skimmed on down the runway and took off, and as the wheels cleared the ground, the blue convertible roared into life and spun around so fast that one wheel dug into a clump of stiff bushes and stopped, dead.

Nodd's face was yellower than ever when we walked over to the place where the coupe was leaning with one front wheel off the ground.

"Top of the morning," said Sam, brightly.

"And much of the same from me," I said, grinning.

He folded over in a faint, and while Sam brought the car, I lugged him out on the grass. Two hours later we were explaining to Chief Holloway and Roller Lester about the new prisoner. In another hour we had the story, or as much as we'd ever get.

Nodd and Denkyn had agreed to get rid of Wenken because he was much too honest for their type of operation. I had been hired as a possible fall guy, and nothing else. Then, when they couldn't get the right sort of cooperation out of me, they had to use Bramlett. Bramlett had been flown there by Dene in the Cessna, a plane he had used going to and fro, from this location to that. After Bramlett killed Wenken, Denkyn wanted to make him take the rap, but Bramlett knew too much, so they had to ride with him. Dene was Bramlett's alibi, so when they were proved together, there it went.

"Bramlett could fly," put in Chief Holloway, a grizzled veteran, another one-time Ranger. "Why did he have to take the girl with him?"

"Probably so they'd have two culprits they could use via the threat method," was Sam's explanation.

Roller messed up his brow with a frown. "Sam, how come you wasn't satisfied with our conclusions that it was Denkyn?"

Sam shrugged expressively. "Just a constitutional antipathy to anything that is as pat as a murderer getting the works himself. Justice isn't always that poetic. However, suspicion of the neat end wasn't the real factor. Frank comes to me with the story, and what crops up but this Dene chick knowing more than she's got any business knowing."

We goggled at him for a moment. I, for one, didn't know what he was talking about.

He looked us over, then smiled at me paternally, almost forgivingly. "What was it she said to you, Frank... the last words?"

I had to think for a moment. "Er ... something about the fact that I was a better ... er, well ..."

"Lover," supplied Sam, gratuitously.

"Yeah," I said, my face as hot as a stove lid. "Then she said she was glad I had quit looking for murderers and said she had Denkyn figured for it all the time. Now, Sherlock, what's so important in that. Several people thought of Denkyn in that light. Me, for one."

Sam nodded tolerantly. "Sure, but where do you suppose Dene got her information? It wasn't public knowledge then. How'd she know you and Roller had given up hunting for murderers? Unless, of course, you told her."

"I didn't tell her ... Holy mackerel ... Well, dammit, how did she know?"

Sam laughed deep in his chest. "I don't know everything. See, Roller, he catches when you rub his nose in it."

They all had a laugh at my expense, then Roller asked me: "What was all that guff she handed you about her sister having been seduced by Denkyn, and she and Dicky were out to get him for it."

"False. Coniver's family was one of those 'your children and my children are fighting our children' setups. Dene and Dicky are brother and sister, but not Coniver's kids. Coniver had three kids by his first wife and two by the second. One, the boy, got toasted to a nice brown in a gas oven by his mother, and she had to be put in a padded cell. Dene and Dicky always hated Coniver. I think the state psychiatrist will find a lot of the old lady in her oldest and next oldest offspring. Dicky, I think, knew enough on Denkyn to make his job secure, and Dene was a handy gal to have around the house for any number of reasons. She and Dicky had enough criminal intent to make them both useful and dangerous. Dene, who is a pretty clever gal, suspected that having me around might be a hazard to her and Dicky. That Denkyn might even use me to get rid of them. That's why she tried to talk me out of the job."

Chief Holloway leaned forward, his eyes a little wolfish. "What do you mean, she was handy to have around the house... the usual?"

"Sure. She was as cute a dish as you'll find in a day's riding. Very, very handy to have around."

Sam grinned. "You should know, pal," and there went my traitorous face again.

The next day was hectic, what with Danessa coming to town, dragging a long, drawn-out gal name of Karrel Chester. Karrel was well named. She was a chester from way back, in spite of her alleged sixteen years of age and, for every blonde wiggle of her head to make her soft hair flash, there was a corresponding wiggle to her body that might start at her ankles and ripple upward, or at the shoulders and ripple downward, making sure that they occurred when I was looking... and I did look. That gal invited rape with every move she made. With this in mind, and the projected dinner and dance at the Shamrock, I invited Sam and Sadie as protection and help.

They helped marvelously, with Sadie taking pity on us by remaining at the table most of the time. We were pretty well spoken for, with Karrel giving me a going over every time we got on the floor, leaving Danessa to Sam. I bore up, but not too well, and when we put them on the bus at twelve midnight, I sighed, told Sam and Sadie goodnight, and took a slow route home. Harem, Prett had called it, but tonight it would be as empty as the last whiskey bottle.

How wrong I was. Prett was sitting on the steps when I drove into the driveway.

"This is no good, kid, all alone here. How long you been waiting?"

"About an hour. I kept calling and no one answered, so I took a taxi out. I have news."

I took her in and, after drinks, I asked: "What's the news?"

"My lawyer hired me anyway," she paused, and looked speculatively into her drink. "I wonder if he knew?"

"Knew what?"

"That his wife had brittle arteries and would throw a fit and bust one."

"What?"

"That's right. He hired me yesterday morning and she simply had a cat. Last night she had a stroke and died this morning at three-thirty."

"*Gad* ... you lethal creature."

"I'm not sorry, Frank." She wasn't, and there was no pretense about it.

"What now?"

She grinned. "I hate work."

"So?"

"Well, I think the man needs a woman about the house."

"No doubt! You?"

"Sure ... me. The kids are big enough to have some sense, and small enough for me to overcome whatever resentment they might have. I think I'll make a good mother, Frank."

All of a sudden I felt an aching knot in my throat. "That's right. You will. I'm going to be married, too."

"The Wenken girl?"

"How'd you know?"

"Every time you mentioned her, your eyes glazed over like a lizard changing color. Is it love, Frank?"

"I guess so. Funny sort of feeling, alright."

"I'm glad ... really glad. You want to take me home now?"

She wore a simple blouse of white, silk or satin (hell, what do I know about such things), and a thin, blue skirt that showed the ridges where her pants gripped her thighs. The blouse showed about everything in the way of straps and supports and whatnot.

"Do you want to go home?"

She smiled. "Eventually."

"Okay ... eventually."

She came to me like a cloud of warm, vitaminized mist, covering me with her clean fragrance and sending thrusts of weakening amperage through me. Her skin was warm, having the smoothness of health and bursting vitality, and her lips were living things in a damp frenzy. She went home ... eventually.

"Dene Coniver came down eventually, and was duly captured," I said, knowing he already knew.

Sam nodded casually. "That always happens when something goes up."

He nibbled a dill pickle with the delicacy of an eastern potentate nibbling a fig. "I wonder," he said, softly, "if you know what you have in Marlo Wenken?"

"No!" I snapped. "You tell me." He had made a trip with me to see how the wedding plans were doing.

"Anhouri, with skin like polished jade; her eyes, jewels, yet uncrystallized; a mind that leaps where other minds crawl. You don't deserve her any more than I do Sadie."

"I'm a salesman. I sold the product."

"Which she will realize, once you've relaxed."

I nodded, but didn't speak.

"Frank, the world is a hell of a place right now. Because of the people in it, I'd better add, since you're given to picayunish retort. Women like Marlo stand revealed in sharp, relieving contrast to the sordid, ugly facets of existence. Don't take her off that ranch. Leave her there … you make the change. You've been used to change, she hasn't. Take her away from what made her as she is, and she might change. Any change you make will necessarily be for the better. Become a rancher and expose yourself to her sun's rays. The results may be salutary."

For once I had no retort—not even a picayunish one—so all I did was breathe an honest: "Amen."